By Fielding Dawson

Stories & Dreams:

Krazy Kat/The Unveiling
The Dream/Thunder Road
The Sun Rises into the Sky
The Man Who Changed Overnight

Novels:

Open Road
The Mandalay Dream
A *Great* Day for a Ballgame
Penny Lane
Two Penny Lane
Three Penny Lane

Novellas:

Elizabeth Constantine
Thread
The Greatest Story Ever Told/A Transformation

Memoirs:

An Emotional Memoir of Franz Kline
The Black Mountain Book (A memoir of the college)

Essays & Criticism:

An Essay on New American Fiction
Entelechy One

Poetry:

Delayed, Not Postponed

THREE PENNY LANE,

A NOVEL

FIELDING DAWSON

SANTA BARBARA
BLACK SPARROW PRESS
1981

3/1981
am Lt Cont

THREE PENNY LANE. Copyright © 1981 by Fielding Dawson.

LIBRARY OF CONGRESS CATALOGING IN PUBLICATION DATA

Dawson, Fielding, 1930-
  Three penny lane.
  I. Title.
PS3554.A948T49   813'.54   80-27344
ISBN 0-87685-447-1
ISBN 0-87685-446-3 (pbk.)

For Painters Everywhere

"The term 'one' does not stand for 'the integral number *one*', which is a complex special notion. It stands for the general idea underlying alike the indefinite article '*a* or *an*', and the definite article '*the*', and the demonstratives '*this* or *that*', and the relatives '*which* or *what* or *how*.' It stands for the singularity of an entity. The term 'many' presupposes the term 'one', and the term 'one' presupposes the term 'many.' The term 'many' conveys the notion of 'disjunctive diversity'; this notion is an essential element in the concept of 'being.' There are many 'beings' in disjunctive diversity.

—Whitehead
Process and Reality

". . . a cycle is just as much a physical metaphor as a flower of Eden; a spiral is just as much a physical metaphor as a precious stone. But, after all, a garden is a beautiful thing; whereas this is by no means necessarily true of a cycle, as can be seen in the case of a bicycle. A jewel, after all, is a beautiful thing; but this is not necessarily so of a spiral, as can be seen in the case of a corkscrew."

—G. K. Chesterton
from his introduction to Dickens'
Christmas Carol, and *The Chimes*
(Penguin, paper)

". . . a little thing affects them. A slight disorder of the stomach makes them cheats. You may be an undigested bit of beef, a blot of mustard, a crumb of cheese, a fragment of an underdone potato. There's more of gravy than of grave about you, whatever you are!"

—Scrooge,
to Marley's Ghost

THREE PENNY LANE

Lucky and Audrey had returned (TWA Flight 700 from Heathrow) from a ten day visit to England to see their friends Andrew and Jean Crozier, who showed them as many of the sights as possible, Andrew having his own writing to do on the spring vacation from teaching, and although Audrey had caught a cold, the trip had been wonderful anyway, save a surprising disappointment—Stonehenge was fenced out by a circle of wire-line inside the circle of stones, so she couldn't wander surrounding fields and gaze upon the great structure.

Yet that disappointment was minor, as the visit had been a dream—they had seen the Giant of Cerne Abbas (no post-cards of him for sure!), so too the Dragone of Uffington, and just before coming home they took a ferry across and spent the day in Dieppe, returning to see, just before sundown, the Long Man of Wilmington.

Thus, after the flight back, they were tired, and while I helped them with their luggage I told Audrey Dottie would call when she (Dottie) got home from work. I then told Lucky we'd see them soon, and as I left they began to unpack, weary but enthusiastic, Audrey sneezing. . . .

We invited them for supper the next night. Lucky gave me a framed reproduction of page 86 of Blake's *Progress of Poesy*, and Dottie got a beautiful red and blue wool scarf, handwoven in Scotland. I suggested Dottie swap with me as she was passionate over Blake and I needed a new scarf, but with wine for the women and Popov for myself and Lucky, the ten-pound turkey with Dottie's incredible mushroom and oyster stuffing, and the rest of the works (cold beer), my boorishness was overlooked, and we spent the rest of the evening listening to their adventures in England. The slides, Audrey said, would be ready next week, and we could all look forward to a show.

It was so good to see Lucky again I couldn't sleep, that night, but around dawn I dropped, as it were, off. Who knows how the unconscious works, my goodness, not I! I dreamed I was in a foreign territory, which seemed like Greece, and yet like South America—Rio? Sitting on a terrace in front of a small cafe which overlooked a bay. I was drinking Stolichnaya 100 and composing a sort of Impressionistic (dare I say?) prose poem, meanderings through San Juan: Rich Port in a coke rico joke with a sentimental end: the Atlantic crashes in, and movie stars shine. Night dark as slavery above a beach stretching out below a hotel balcony, night like El Creep de mal Franco, luminous silver haze against blue so deep it could be black, in which I saw a form, a cloud-shape—Lucky's profile! his eyes sprang out of a hole in the white veil, towards the Sheraton.

This—so this is love. We laughed tonight, witty and bright, light in ourselves, so good to be me and you came across the sky in your cloud, you *knew* I would see in Stoly Juan / overlooking the bay / easy to say (this way), I can't remember, yet as the tip of your nose crossing palm trees—a tickle:

The humor in being a bone
is being along alone
a bone,
along the beach too gone
to gnaw

BUT!

When the stars fell
we watched the dancers dance
I heard trumpets
—scarlet silence

As beginnings go, Lucky said, that's pretty good. A cloud like me, eh? I feel like Pooh.

A mere dream, Ratty, said I, and on the swing of the narrative to you, my dear, I'd like it if you'd write that Blaze came in here in dirty blue and green plaid Bermuda shorts, a worn white Brooks Brothers shirt, bare feet in deck sneakers, and under his burnished copper curls, his face shone as a pink sun.

Nobody wears plaid Bermuda shorts anymore, Lucky said, but burnished copper curls is a cliché I like, against, no above the pink sun, all right, okay, I'll think about it.

He sipped vodka.

I had helped him and he had helped me, with laundry and shopping. We'd taken our carts, so we sat in our usual places with our carts full of groceries and clean laundry, while Lucky briefed Frank on England—Frank not altogether enlightened, for Lucky had said little to enlighten, England is green, everyone everywhere hates the English, including the Scots, Welsh and to be sure, the Irish, so the English, along with the rest of the world that hates Americans, hate Americans, and as both countries are going broke, a kinda nexus is formed, although the bars in London are no good, just as the bars in Goof City, Brighton on Sundays is a rush hour anywhere. Bobbies are called cops, or fuzz, and the pubs have become bars, nobody says downtown or uptown or midtown, they say centre.

I had known all this, of course, from my lecture tours, but enjoyed Lucky getting a laugh out of Frank saying how small England is, from London to Glasgow not so far as from Goof to Buff, as characters began drifting into the bar for the cocktail hour, we got our material goods together, and before we said farewell, we had one—just one—each, a little one to the brim, on Frank, for our journey homeward.

***

The next day I received a manuscript in the mail, and upon opening the envelope and reading the cover letter, I thought Lucky should see it, for it was a work of prose. Yet the letter was interesting, and it was only after I read the
"You might not remember me, but—"
drift, plus the information given, as well as the name, that I did remember him, and he said he would be in town the following Marsday, three away, so I decided Lucky and I should get together and read the manuscript, so that I (and maybe we), could be prepared. I had a hunch that the story would be good—he'd been a fine writer, his first novel very impressive but being slow in sales, died. On the strength of his advance he had gotten married, and in spite of the danger of writers teaching he had gotten an assistant professorship at a WeCo College but with the cutbacks, was fired, his wife left him, and he was at present on unemployment and working at finishing his second novel, manuscript enclosed, with

apologies knowing the poet was busy, but any suggestions would be appreciated.

I called Lucky, who was having breakfast saying it would be better if I visited him, rather than he me, as he had so much housework to do he couldn't get away, even to the bar, until it was done. I said I had to do much of the same myself, and we agreed I should call him when I was through. I did, he said come on over, and I did, manuscript in hand.

Do you remember Joe Jo? I asked, as I went in, Lucky holding the door for me.

In. He closed the door. Sure, he said. Get back, Jo-jo! That the guy?

I forgot, I said, to note in my poem from my dream that I had whistled *Summer Sequence* on the way to the hotel.

Hotel?

You're so hard to see!

We sat down. At his desk, which he had cleaned up. I took the manuscript out of the envelope and we sat close together, picked up pencils, and looked at the title page of *The Painter Nathan Fierce*, turned the page and read the opening sentence, which was—Guys liked her.

"This is it."

"Right."

Guys liked her. She was easy to talk with, she liked to drink, smoke dope, gossip and screw *when* (she stressed), she wanted.

"Solotaroff would cut that italic and the paren," said Lucky.

"Indeed," said I, feeling worldly. To also read (as best she could), and be herself. She was a young artist searching out her life in (then), her third year of college.

"Do we know this story?"

"By heart. Or—do we?"

Her straight brown hair was parted in the middle, and

15

curved in at the neck. She had steady level brown eyes, an upturned nose with flared nostrils, and Jane Fonda lips.

"I'm getting that Bugs and Flap feeling."

"Me too. The 3rd Baseline Bar."

She loved to laugh, talk and chew gum, and her lips, as she chewed moved in a sensual way that invited, in an easy quick sense, men as friends, although duration exceeded depth. She also liked candy—sweets, as she said (the German in her).

"German?"

"German. That's what it says."

"He wrote."

The French came out when she got her period, and along avec ça, le acne, right out in the open, and she suffered even behind her face, got agitated, which seemed to create a voice ordering her to be bitchy.

"No!"

She wore mountain climber's boots, jeans and faded blue chambray shirts. She held her head high, her back straight, and with long rapid strides moved through city traffic the way a farm girl moves through corn.

"That's good," Lucky said, "but I hope it isn't the best line in the book, because we're still on page one."

"Read on," I advised. "We can rewrite later."

"Who said anything about rewriting?"

"I did."

"You mean you think I was about to?"

I nodded.

"I wasn't," Lucky said.

"I feared you were. You're being irrational."

"I am. Aren't you?"

"We are."

"Joyce Carol Oates doesn't rewrite."

"She doesn't write to rewrite."

"How do you know?"

"Read her books."

"I'm getting thirsty."

"Me too. Shall we plough on?"

We read she had, in a modern style of speaking away from associations, a remarkable common sense, yet it was also remarkable that she could be so dense. Her love of secrets, which verged on passion, coupled with her passion for gossip, brought out the French in her, as well as the fool, in the way one feels at the fork in the road, a suspense as in being fascinated, knowing secrets and the freshest gossip, but ignorant of how she sounded when she imitated the voices of secrets and those of gossip, when she spoke, as well as the face she wore as she spoke, and assumed in her eagerness to hear more—"sweets."

"Right."

Thirty years before she would have worn bangs, frills, and jumpers, and often when he looked at her, he thought he saw—they laughed about it—well, maybe! he admitted, it was his projection, of what he wanted her to be. Not what she was, to which she agreed, not without anger. Some things which seem so clear may, in the transparency, also seem invisible. For himself, at least, he grew to understand her in the way he could see her, which was his undoing, because when she left him, she took all he could see with her,—all her invisibles along with her face, and her body, the most visible person he saw, had seen, leaving him with empty hands holding an invisible mirror, or a mirror in which he only saw himself, for it was as if she had never been in his mirror. But she found other hands, to hold and see her scrubbed face, sparkling teeth, glossy hair combed in such a mysterious girl-way an odd reflecting glow hung suspended, and in silent benediction murmured *You look fine*. See the drawing dawning nuance, nimbus Nebula there, to bind the spell, Nance?

"I do."

"So do I. He's describing girls with mirrors as if they were a phenomenon."

"Well, they sure are. Did you help him write this?"

He was teasing me again.

"No, did you?"

"No. You know him, I don't. It reads a little like you."

"Ah well, it reads like you as well." I smiled like a cat. Lucky likes that.

You think I do, he thought, you vodka-soaked egotist. Me!

"Nancy," Lucky read aloud, "with her natural Westworld look, didn't need cosmetics, except when she had—"

Do you have any beer?

And?

—nevertheless, she was, in her spell, shrewd in a selection of her faces, this comes later—to reflect the way she wanted to be seen as she selected which one of the boys at the bar to be with. It was as if by plan, she thought, not knowing she was in another plan, on the lookout to all appearances, but underneath governed by whims and wills no one saw, and he almost did, but couldn't believe it, it was so clear, that what was going on behind her face were voices directing her to select an attitude for each appropriate face, so no matter where she went or what she did, she did what she wanted which she was told to do, loved gossip, the expression on her face was a face and the tone of heard gossip reflected and even echoed the tenor of her inner voices, and the secrets she (as they) loved, yet no one must know (they said). That was law. So when which face heard what secret, or confessed one, in the day by day gossip at her job or at the bar with other faces quite like hers, yet did that matter? Her voices listened, and curious or not, in speaking to her she fixed a face, listening, for they sounded as the voices at the bar.

"I bet that spooked her."

"Him. Not her."

Which was why she feared the unexpected, true surprise, because it upset her directed preparations. She prepared for any outward event, responses ready, face set, corresponding attitude alert and the field of action smooth before her. Quick surprise made her speechless, unnerved, near tears.

In a throwaway line she told him it was easy for her to cry, and long after he could imagine the voice that told her to tell him that, which might have been a clue to why she thought truths were strange, *So, it's true!* she felt adult in the telling, she put on a face for it, how strange to be adult! causing her to laugh at, she thought, herself, which delighted her, leaving aside what or who caused her to laugh, which perplexed her, for she had felt vague, and on the verge of being contrary. This of course was when she was living in town, and twenty-two.

"What the hell is that?"

"Chili," Lucky said, and as he went into the kitchen to stir it, I sipped Bud, and thought about this story of cracked-up identification. Maybe that's what infatuation is—complete identification with another, total departure from one's self into the life of the cherished, worshipped other, and to love with the love one needs for oneself. To love

and to cherish until Death do us—

in: we looked at each other, but as if from the touch of unseen hands, our heads swiveled to the manuscript—words sprang into focus.

The fun with secrets and gossip—a sort of tactical espionage she enjoyed at the bar—sustained and exercised her voices, which she believed in her name because she was practical, after all, with the boys there her common-sense adult-seeming face and personality was cover for a greedy uncaring artist itself, which meant, in the company of those nice guys, whom in part she wanted to be, in boots, pants, and work-shirts, if she couldn't be one of them, she could be a friend, a mascot, reliable in her own body and, it occurred even to her, although perhaps in a shudder, that she could manipulate them from that angle. Sustaining herself while keeping her controlling voices happy—or at bay—following their orders and the rule, yet feeling uncomfortable because she too was being used, but then, that too was part of it. She knew what give and take meant. She also knew when she was safe, a sweet girl who could be trusted, a pal, someone you can count on, good people—these form an image. She was a warm young person at the old bar, and the boys sitting around were glad to see her. Although from another point of view, as even they watched her careful invasion into their bar, to be one of them, causing some to feel avuncular toward her, others felt more than a cool merriment, and their language fit a more conventional narrative. But in secret, even so, she merged her inner voices with theirs, as if to manipulate the whole bar as a body of the voices she needed—her voices needed, overlook-ing the juke box and through the window the slanting city street beyond, over all hovered the sound of Dracula herself, yearning for voices to feed no one must know, that for a pleasant uncle, or, an ambitious young critic, that for just a (few words) little voice, the boys could feed off her, too,— they might get a surprise! for a while, until the freshness vanished, which was inevitable, so the nice guys were more quiet, the others more noisy, one by one she'd used them, and it came to pass that strangers became voices to hear, yet it was too transient, the sound was muddled, and in a difficult awareness she found difficult to understand, she felt a fright deeper than anything she'd understood—what should she do? Find a new bar? There weren't any new bars. They were all

20

one big place: a joint in which to guzzle, talk and get out of. Empty-eyed she poured Scotch and soda into a mouth of stone, unable to grasp what was going on. Drear and empty in mind and body, she couldn't understand that every once in a while even the sound of Dracula fell still.

"You stir the chili and I'll pour Popov."

I did, he did, and we stood in Lucky's kitchen looking at each other.

"To Bram Stoker," I smiled.

"To the author of this story," said Lucky. "This guy cares too much, chasing her down fiction-alley, preoccupied with his own obsession, do you think he'll let her go?"

"She went," in a sudden yeah! yeah! yeah! we drank to *Penny Lane*, in memory, John Lennon.

BAM!

"Where's that passage when she comes to town and he introduces her to everybody as his spiritual sister?"

"How do you know that?" Lucky asked.

"My secret," I said. "He finds her a beautiful loft in a good neighborhood. The rent is low and it has a roof where she can sunbathe. And later, when she's troubled and too innocent to know what to do, he gets her a top therapist."

Yes. She'd made the insertion of d in between the *o* and *y* of boy, though Madame X didn't know it, and I wrote what I saw while the young one did what I witnessed, and of my responses to her. If I hadn't I couldn't respond to my writing or to me. I'd be less than I am and the story dispassionate, a pretension or a long and dirty lie, but anger is none of those things, and if my anger doesn't fit understood facts then the facts must suffer me. If I'd write the truth of her as she is seen by others I wouldn't have enough prose to put on a postcard, or just enough—perhaps the accurate description of her at the beginning of this. She was a young artist new to the city, she followed her destiny—she: as pungent as 3.2 beer, subtle as truth twice told.

But when I was with her, in her studio loft, and we were surrounded by her paintings and things, and we talked, I kept seeing different faces in her face—even there! away from the bar!—and I heard other voices, although it was she I was with, yet she seemed in flashes I couldn't believe I saw: fluid, static, happy, confused, distracted, doubtful, considerate, selfish but concerned, tight-lipped, arrogant, ambitious, humble, uncaring, determined, dreamy, willful, impulsive, manipulative, and in under her practical artistic self, green and greedy. It seemed a lot of quarreling was going on inside, little of which showed on her face except when it did, like a split in custard, and I had the feeling she was being used. As if something was feeding in on her body home, turning her around and about this way and that, feeding on her, standing there beneath her skylight, the way it linked to the bar as the door opened and her body went in as if it was her, to her, jabbering racket of guys, television, the jukebox, pinball machines, and kitchen noises—voice was her medium, not vision—in a blur of color standing under her skylight at home, it was a shame she wasn't great. What was going on in there had real potential. But because I was infatuated I couldn't see, as clear as the skylight above, that in her true, yet manipulated denial of love (she admitted she didn't know what love was (is that why she could weep at will?), the nance revealed one afternoon in a voice I'd not heard so far, as she turned on me—following a piece of advice I'd given to her—lips parted—

You're getting too close!

I didn't hear her. I'd become too dependent on her, and she knew it as well as I didn't want to admit it, and she knew that too, for she was clever, and had she seen that! she might have been interesting.

As I was, but I was a fool, a fact which she understood to

the point of my disgusting her. How could I have expected a twenty-two year old girl/woman to hold up a forty-five year old drunkard coming off a bad divorce and very heavy, leaning on her? But what else do middle-aged and infatuated characters expect? I needed her no, not love, yes perhaps a little, but in all her body, wasn't it mine? hadn't I given her—as if a visual body was departing from my dreamer's ken, as in a dream, a nuance of us governed my mind from which she withdrew, to the high road of her own life, along the bonnie colonnades, locales, northwest corners painting and drawing, breathing, living and in a dream without dreams in Paradise City, to the guys of the bar and the world become somebody, a popular person, and leave the incestuous dreamer behind. Who was getting too close. So. I was too blind to help myself, and in my fantasy, not once having seen her as she was, save the certainty that she was a good painter, in the illusion of art I presumed she was mine. I had, after all—when she arrived in town— introduced her to my friends in my bars as my spiritual sister.

There.

Lucky looked at me, ran his hand through his hair and said, "This story is as old as the hills. Why didn't he write a poem and have done with it?"

"If it happened to you, would you?" I asked.

"It depends."

"On what."

"My mood," he said, riffling the many pages of the manuscript. "What do you think?"

" 'The chatter, the laughter!' " I cried.

Began to belong, yet somehow it was familiar, in the subtle home games she began anew to know. On the long distance calls to and from her folks, I heard her voice change depending on who she was talking to. Cautious with Dad, Mom the ear for confidential woman-talk, therefore voice of diplomatic, enthusiastic obedience with him, and secret whisper gossip personal with her. A concerned adult with her brother, he being younger, a geewhiz little girl with her grandparents, and understanding modern woman with her younger sister, all so habitformed the voices verged on personalities, and in the bar—the chatter, the laughter! began to belong, yet somehow—it had never been so clear last year, in school, or before at home, a form was coming into being which in outline resembled her, but in composition was almost invisible, as she. Talking was her game, and although from a familiar threshhold her horizons were widening—she was meeting new faces—she was apprehensive, because if all this freshness happened so fast with so little effort, as if from ambush, would her voices sustain her for the inevitable future moves she'd have to make? What would they be? How would she make them?

The direct language she'd learned from her college teacher didn't work in the city, and after having been direct, at first, she quit fast. Began a linguistic cleanup campaign. Was a friend to all, stayed in control and smoothed out the rough patches she'd made. The boys liked it, aw yeah—she was fun! Diplomatic, empathetic, adult, young, game, and in a tight spot a figure of amelioration, she worked herself into popularity, or, a viable fabric flexible enough for the bar, the city and the world until it all fit. Not bad, oh no, yet this distributing, watering down and creating an acceptable pattern had the spooky quality as integrity compromised always does, of someone following somebody else's orders, manipulating true emotions to sustain an accepted image was as if her personality had been turned inside out—just as instructed. So the pleasant, rational young woman having a drink after work, in the cocktail chatter of the day she was from a wide view almost enviable, except something was missing, or, in a chilly perception, was the implant malfunctioning? for when she was spoken to in terms of ideas, or of certain conclusions having been arrived at from having thought of certain things, or of her opinions concerning personalities, say of a friend who was a painter, who liked her work but she didn't like his, her eyes changed, got a raw mica look until she got instructions on which voice to speak, her eyes cleared, focused, and she responded: firm and lucid. A second before, there had been something hollow.

And if one looked close, and steady, one saw her face had changed. When questioned she had looked baffled, distracted, and in an eerie sense, *as if made simple*. The voice-jolts she got from persons asking her questions beyond the chatter could almost paralyze her, and she became confused, as one who generalizes is by a quick particular. She worked hard to control her face, make a mask to cover her vulnerability to surprise and the spontaneous. In a close-up of her, the pleasant, rational young woman having a drink after work, what appeared to be an introspective look, or a look of considering a thought, one would in fact see a protruding lower lip, veiled eyes, and an expression about to drool. The mask had slipped. Thank God for her acne. It brought her back to life. I'm a writer. I watch people.

That I no longer mattered didn't itself matter, except to me, and that didn't matter to her, for she had smoothed her exit over in a way that told me she was forming her life by compromise, at twenty-three in the guise of honesty: she built an identity that worked. She was a nice person.

In our last factual conversation, she spoke to my face in the mirror behind the bar in another joint, across town. Her face was as pale and mask-like as certain faces in *Les Enfants*, and her manipulative arrogance as clear as cable tv, she informed my face there in the mirror, that she was going to "take it all." She wouldn't tell the bartender or a painter she admired, because she was telling me goodbye, and the cruel excitement was on her face, and the voice was one of absolute command. Out in the open at last, that voice which had warned me I was getting too close, so I was out in the open at last, too, on the day before Valentine's, I watched her finish her drink, stand up, say she'd keep in touch because she wanted to remain friends. She turned, walked to the front door, opened it, and walked out of my life.

"She's very young," said Madame X, to me.
True.

But.

I write from my vision and my experience, and I respond to the whatness of that vision, and that experience, not to what is true. I will be as true as possible in my work and my life, to me and to thee, yet in all truth more to me than thee, and in the highest truth of all, I will be most true to this.

My drunken irrationality was too much for her. I was out of control while she fought for it. I was involved in my problems and she with her behavior. Why should she need me? except to smooth things out for her. I did a lot of that, while she manipulated me and I let her. So I too, just as she, fell enthralled to her controllers. Obeying orders I fell victim to her body, as she to her voices—they reckoned: All right, why not use him? He is, after all, asking for it. Tell him you want to be alone—tell him you want your own adventure, to live your own life, tell him you want to be friends. Tell him you don't think it's a good idea to have sex anymore because you don't want to hurt him. That's direct, and sounds adult. Tell him it isn't because of any other guy—that's true enough, and useful besides. If you do it right, he might help you out—ha ha! What a *guy!*

You'll forget him—we will. Don't worry. Remember, you have his letters and a lot of his personal secrets. No, you won't tell anyone (isn't that what we all say?), but it's all good to have! Why be guilty? You wouldn't even think of it! Look, if you're going to get where we want you to get, listen to us. When his pride was hurt you said you wanted to be his friend—you did your best. Feels good, knowing that.

To hell with him. Find a guy your own age anyway. Okay, a little older. Also, get real busy painting. In a couple of years we want you to exhibit—he was right in encouraging you, but he was not and is not of us, nor will he ever be. He tried, and failed. He's different. He's too much himself. Keep your eyes and ears open. There are guys who can help you. You're free. You're your own person, you know what to do, we'll tell you the way, you're ours, you can do anything we want and we're out to win. We're free! Don't worry about Madame X, either. We'll take care of her. When she goes on vacation this summer, you'll miss her, sure you will, maybe, but we'll handle you. We understand. Have fun, pretend to think things over. We don't want you to get too serious with her. It's easy for you to cry, so keep crying. It looks good. Shrinks like it, that's why they have boxes of Kleenex around—forget her. Hurry! Wash and fix your face again. There's the mirror. That's the girl. Plain, expectant, cautious, but clever. To the bar! Brush your teeth. Let's go! We're thirsty!

*

FADE IN:

EXT. EXTREME L.S. OF
MANHATTAN ROOFTOPS   DAY
The West 14th-23rd Street area.
                                            CUT TO:

EXT. L.S. OF LOFT BUILDINGS.   DAY

                                            CUT TO:
EXT. M.L.S. OF ONE ROW   DAY
OF LOFT BUILDING WINDOWS
Domestic objects and large paintings
are seen inside.

Music: Mussorgsky: *Pictures at an*
Exhibition.
                                            DISSOLVE TO:

INT. LOFT: CLOSE UP OF PAINT
WALL
A table stands before it with paint
pots, brushes, a staple gun, on top. A
large blank canvas is stapled onto the
paint wall.

Music rises.
                                            CUT TO:

INT. LOFT: THE BLANK CANVAS
FILLS THE SCREEN
The tip of a wide brush begins to

paint, dipping off screen for more
paint, in bright colors with the blunt
elegance of Kline's signature, the
letters in that style:

FILLING THE SCREEN:
    THE PAINTER NATHAN FIERCE

                                     DISSOLVE TO:

A BLACK SCREEN
with white letters:
    The Second Tuesday in February

                                       DISSOLVE TO:

INT. THE SAME LOFT: NIGHT
DESERTED
except for the most minimal furniture and the large paint wall, on
which two huge paintings are
stapled, yet they are dim in the distance. NATHAN FIERCE faces his
ex-wife ALICE. A valise is at Alice's
feet.

                    NATHAN
        Here, I'll carry your bag down.

                    ALICE
    You always were good in the little things.

He picks up the bag, and they walk

to the door.

EXT. STREET   NIGHT
It is snowing.
A VW bus, loaded with furniture
and plants, is parked by the curb. At
the wheel is JAKE, and beside him,
his wife ARLENE, both tightlipped.

CUT TO:

INT. VW BUS CLOSE UP PROFILE
SHOT OF ARLENE AND JAKE
as beyond Jake, a street door opens
and Nathan and Alice appear.
Nathan hands Jake the valise and
Jake puts it in the back.

                    NATHAN
            Thanks, Jake.
                    JAKE
            Sure Nathan.

Nathan and Alice walk around the
bus, and as Arlene slides over, Alice
gets in, closes the door and rolls
down the window. She has tears
in her eyes.

                    ALICE
            Take care, Nathan.

30

NATHAN
I will, dear—you too.

Jakes starts the engine. Nathan steps
back.

NATHAN
Tell the kids I'll see them soon.

ALICE
(murmurs)
Sure.

She rolls up the window and the bus
drives down the street. Nathan
stands, watching it go.

NATHAN
Fifteen fucking years.

DISSOLVE TO:

*

I have to shop, Lucky said. Mario and Helen are coming for supper. We'll finish tomorrow.

Okay, I said. See you later—

Audrey told me this morning, take it easy today—don't get trapped at the bar with Blaze.

"You won't," I quoted, taking off my glasses which I'd put on to impress him.

We, I said, are inviting Max and Seymour tonight, those dear bachelors, and Dottie has instructed me, I might add in no uncertain tones, to avoid getting paralyzed with my Luckiest love at the bar. I smiled.

It's a plot, Lucky smirked—not a happy expression—practically.

A good story, he said.

Which one? I grinned.

You know what I mean, Blaze said, making a threatening gesture—to put his glasses back on so he could look at me, in that way. Like Churchill with no brandy.

Okay, I know what you mean. Yes, but look, as I have some work to do, and only a little shopping, why don't we take it easy and meet at the bar later than usual?

He looked out the window, and said good. The shadow on that office building hasn't yet touched the cornice, which means I have a chance to type up an essay—shall I call you?

Swell—in fact when I get finished, I'll call you.

We'll call each other, he smiled, rising and gathering the manuscript in his hands. I too stood, and we walked to the door together, I opened it, we said so long and I watched him walk down the steps, then closed the door, went into the kitchen, panfried a large centercut pork chop, heated leftover lentils, made a small lettuce, tomato, cucumber and radish salad with oil and tarragon vinegar and when all was ready, I sat at the big table and enjoyed my lunch.

Afterward I propped myself up on my bed, and proceeded

to correct the manuscript of a new, and most amazing novel which put me to sleep. I woke to a ringing telephone, glanced at that, the most foolish machine ever made, put my manuscript to one side, rolled over and picked up the receiver of another foolish machine saying it was two two knowing it was Blaze, and—was he excited! saying the guy who'd written the story was in town and wants himself and me to hear his notes toward a script for a movie—

I'd been asleep for two hours.

I'll meet you in a half-an-hour, I said, and we said see you then, hung up. I rose, put the manuscript on the table by the bed, shaved, brushed my teeth, and with the shopping list, I left, did my chores and met Blaze at the bar with his friend whose name I can't pronounce but who was as excited as a girl in a Victorian novel—blue eyes a little frantic, but very bright, and his round cheeks, high forehead and whole enthusiastic face was flushed with an egotism I liked. He was tall, slender, in his late thirties, balding with rosebud lips in a peajacket, white shirt open at the collar, light grey pleated slacks, light blue cotton socks, and dark tan loafers.

I'm going to dedicate it to Jackson Pollock, he said. His voice was soft, and warm in a way one might call cool.

I expressed my good response and wished him luck, adding that Blaze and myself had enjoyed his story, had read it carefully—and did what writers often do with each other, quoted certain passages and mention their context. The title, too, I said, that's great—*Nancy*, I coughed, *Drew in Paradise*. His face softened and he put out his hand which I took, and we clasped hands, and as he spoke I was a little embarrassed by his compliments and, in his soft cool way, mentioning in return in-context details, and while looking square in my eyes, he smiled and quoted a couple of words and sentences that, he said, had influenced him. He was proud to meet me, and would mention me in Hollywood—which I vetoed.

—Don't. Not until you know you won't be in a charitable mood.

How then?

If they ask, I said.

He lowered his eyes and frowned like a girl, but looked up, made a bitter smile, saying I get it. If they ask, I'll know they're not interested in me.

Yes. But that's one way they'll let you know, most likely they'll just tell you straight out. They'll be decent about it, and be open to future work you think they might like—which won't mean a thing, as you know. But anyway, no mention of me. This is your show. When you're rolling in dough and famous, and hear of something Paramount's got going, you might drop a name, and until then thanks, anyway, let's have a drink, and while Blaze was saying nice things to me about me I looked down the bar to Frank, who was talking with a black detective and a blonde waitress, but who turned, and in a moment we had three fresh drinks.

The bar was quiet. A few couples were finishing up their lunches, and the waitresses and busboys were cleaning up, so as we stood at the far end of the bar, with the jukebox silent and WNCN bringing muted classics to us, the background was perfect. The winter sun shone through the front window, and across the Avenue beyond, the sky was blue above the park. Traffic rushed along.

Goof City was humming.

Right here, but should I read it to you? It's long, and besides, I could tell it to you. I have it, he tapped the side of his head—up here.

Me too, of mine: read on.

34

Blaze said well, in a rather hurt voice, I know my poems by heart—

Eek you, I said and he looked at me, eyebrows arched: reading, he queried, Joyce by chance?

Chaucer, I replied. Shall we listen?

Blaze's friend asked if we wanted to know the storyline, or the general idea etc.,—It's along the same lines as—

I held up my hand with Blaze, and the talker stopped talking, with a shy grin. I said—

Read it from the beginning. No what-it's-about, please. Just the story. No why-it-was-written, or where, or if it's any good, or isn't, the story will tell us all we want to know, and if it's a good one we'll know all we need to know. A lot of writers never understand that when they relate their stories it's the story that wants to be heard, and while poets burst into verse, writers insist on explaining—

But it's about a well-known painter in his mid-fifties who's broke, and—you, yes, okay. You're right. And listen, I know I'm projecting, it's about me, but I can't help it, and besides, so what? Isn't the matter the story? I—I heard so deep I saw—

The talker paused, to Blaze's considered admonishment: Please. Okay, he resumed, with a chuckle, opening a spring bound cover and revealing snow white paper, the pages of which he turned until he found the first—it opens, he began, in a farewell in snowfall, the second Tuesday in February of that year, at around eight p.m. The artist, Nathan Fierce is facing his ex-wife Alice—Alice Weaver Fierce.

Fierce? questioned Blaze. Isn't that a little—corny?

I like it, I said.

It has to be, the storyteller said, it's a corny story.

Dramatic corn at that, Blaze remarked to himself. Fierce—well, poet, be still, let the story continue!

Actually she had divorced him the day before, and tonight

she's moving into an apartment upGoof that she's sublet from friends who have gone to Europe.

Nathan and Alice had been married, though separated often, for around fifteen years. Had children late. The children are already in the new apartment, waiting for Alice, as south of them Nathan and Alice face each other in no longer theirs, but Nathan's big loft, which is almost empty as everything of hers is gone—clothes, desk, chairs, the rocker, books, plants, etc., yet there is more packed into the VW bus which is parked on the street below. The loft looks as forlorn as the two people who had shared it. She writes her telephone number on a slip of paper and hands it to him, saying—

Here's my phone number. I have to go. Jake and Arlene are waiting.

I know, he says, here, I'll carry your bag down.

Thank you, you were always good in the little things.

He picks up a valise and they go out the door, down the steps onto the sidewalk in the snow. Nathan hands the valise to Jake, at the wheel, whose wife Arlene is in the front seat beside him. She leans forward to see Nathan as Jake puts the valise in the back. Nathan says,

Listen Jake, I'm really grateful.

I know you are, Jake responds, not quite hostile, but not all so warm. Yet understanding.

Nathan has a haggard hurt look and walks around the bus with Alice, as Arlene opens the door, and slides across the seat to Jake. Nathan and Alice embrace in the street, holding each other close.

Take care sweetheart, she says. Tears in her eyes.

I will, dear—you too. Tears in his eyes.

They part, step back and look at each other. She gets in the bus, closes the door, rolls down the window and looks out at him. Jake starts the engine.

Goodbye Alice, Nathan murmurs, tell the kids I'll see

them soon.

As she lowers her head her farewell is scarcely audible, and as she rolls up the window the machine backs up, and then pulls out heading east. Nathan stands in the street watching it go, looking forlorn and anxious. But then he goes back upstairs, stands inside his loft and looks around.

Fifteen years, he mutters—flashback: he's working on a very large painting. She's in the rear of the loft, at her typewriter, writing. Debussy's *Preludes* are being played on the stereo. A cat is asleep on a rug near Alice's feet. Two children, a boy and a girl, are asleep in beds in a far corner. The loft, home to them all, is very large, and made beautiful by his paintings, her plants, his drawings and their photographs, wall hangings, letters and postcards from friends around the world, museum and gallery announcements, book and art reviews and photos of Nathan and Alice together here and overseas, plus the dust jacket of her first novel, plus drawings and visual gifts from other painters, etc. He lowers his paint brush, looks at the canvas, and with brush in hand crosses the floor to her. She turns, and glances up at him.

How's it going? he smiles.

Tough, she says. Go away.

He walks away saying over his shoulder: Same here, crosses toward his bed, sits, picks up the telephone, dials a number and waits.

Across town, down on the vastside, a plain, pretty woman with a slightly pockmarked face in her early twenties comes out of a brightly lit loft into a hallway. She is wearing jeans, a chambray shirt and sneakers which all have paint on them. As she picks up the receiver she stands in a bright shaft of light, from the open door behind her, and in part silhouette, she says hello.

Hi, Nathan says.

Hi, listen, I'm painting—can you—

37

Can I come over?

Sure, but call first—in about two hours, okay?

Okay. Alice and the kids are gone. Divorced yesterday, gone today. The loft is a shell.

How are you feeling?

Frightened, and dreadful.

Aw Nathan—

Okay, see you later, Work well.

I'll try. Thanks. Bye.

She hangs up, and went down the hallway into another bright, spotless white studio with a polished hardwood floor where a rigid young woman artist stood at a sink, washing her hands. Minimal objects were placed at seeming random on the floor and walls. She looked up as Judy came in, and asked,

How's he doing?

Frightened. I don't know what to do. He's coming over in a while. Do you have any cigarettes?

No. When?

Couple hours.

Well friend, what's to say? You've let it get serious to a point where you—

I know, Judy interrupted, looking worried. I wish I knew what love was.

The other artist made a sardonic smile, and said That's a twist. Then, added—Look, Judy, he's not so important. There are guys more your age you ought to be seeing, who are doing up-to-date stuff, and not that fifties shit, and you—

But that isn't true! Judy cried. I know your voice! He's following his—his—his own process, development, he hasn't stopped—

Yeah. Motherwell & co. I know. But Nathan's more than twice your age—

I know, Judy sighed, and yeah, okay and maybe, etc., but I need him, and he sure needs me, old-fashioned or not, that guy is *alive.*

The other artist shrugged, and dried her hands as Judy left to phone Nathan to bring some smokes.

I lit the storyteller's filter, my Gauloises after Blaze's, and we sipped our drinks, myself and Blaze looking at each other as we began to get the drift, smiling, as the storyteller did too, seeing our expressions, nodded, said okay, you're getting it. It's four nights later, *The Explosion on Valentine's Eve.* God! I hope they see it!

In candlelight. She stretches her naked young body, yawns, and turning to Nathan (naked too), says, with warmth,

Gee, that was great.

He lights a cigarette and hands it to her, and as she puffs from it, she adjusts the pillow behind her so that she's sitting up. He does the same, so they're both sitting up in her bed, leaning into pillows against the wall.

He puts his arm around her and she rests her head on his shoulder, both suddenly thoughtful. He sips his drink.

What day is this? she asks.

Dawn of Friday, he answers, and says, shaking his head, Jesus, it's been four days since she divorced me, and three since it hit me. Tomorrow's Valentine's day—be my Valentine?

She frees herself, and turning, sits so she is facing him, and speaks:

Listen, Nathan, no—I—she pauses, takes a deep breath, and cries, I want some adventure! I want to *do* things!

Great! he laughs—me *too.* Where do we go? we're broke!

She looks at him, and she is as a different person, with a calm, cruel expression, saying—

I'm going to be honest with you. Our involvement is over. I want to be on my own.

He—sits up turning to her, and says, in panic—

But where—his hands are visibly shaking—am I? Not every man loses his wife and mistress in four days for Christ's *sake* Judy! What about *me?*

She lowers her head, then raises it, and speaks, looking in his eyes—

I don't know. We'll have to work it out. We'll see each other, of course, but—

His face—like a direct hit in war—explodes, yet his words are clear.

But what in hell is going on? What in *hell* is going on? I need you!

She then becomes a little frightened, and puts her hand on his shoulder in a slight—apprehension, and says, as to smooth things out, yet with an undertone of condescension—

I know you do. Look, it isn't like it sounds, it isn't because of another guy or other guys, it's just that I—

He leaps on her and begins kissing her breasts and belly while embracing her buttocks with one arm and her shoulders with the other. Suddenly he pulls away, looks at her in terror, jumps up, and his face bleached, stammers, stares across her loft, his body jerks, he moves to the ladder of the raised platform on which her bed is, goes down the ladder fast, gets into his clothes muttering to himself, buttons, zips, tucks in and while tying his shoelaces, speaks fast—

I don't know what's going on, but I can't take it—I'm going! I'll call you tomorrow Jesus fucking CHRIST Judy!

She is then a very frightened girl, eyes wide, lips trembling as Nathan gets into his coat, and, as he heads for the door, says over his shoulder—

Oh good*night* Judy God *damn*—

Nathan! she cries—wait! but he is gone from her loft, and his footsteps recede down the corridor, followed by the distant sound of a door closing. She collapses on her bed, and buries her face in the pillow.

Really, Blaze said, only those who know, know these things happen on birthdays, Christmas, New Year's etc.,—

You'd think she would have known, too, smiled the story-teller—grim.

The End of A Candy Heart the next day, at an anonymous bar, Nathan is seated alone, anxious and depressed, frowning and muttering to himself. Judy comes in and sits next to him. They kiss and exchange awkward greetings and his hand trembles as he gives her a large red candy heart, saying—

I don't know if I should give you this, in view of last night, but after you called today I got it for you, so here it is in an anyway sense. You took the real one, so take this one too. Frame it, like a metaphor—a frame-up. Lick it. Suck it. Eat it. Fuck it.

I'm sorry, she says, taking the candy without looking at it. I didn't—I didn't think you'd be so upset.

Then, like peering around a corner afraid of what she might see—

We'll still be friends.

He picks up his drink, but his hand is shaking so badly he lowers the drink to the bar, puts both hands around it, raises it to his lips and drains it, turns to her, and asks—

That means what I think it means?

I want to be your friend! she cries, but her face changes. From eagerness she becomes objective and benevolent, and her words come out as in a direct line of a different, but premeditated attack:

I don't want to hurt you, Nathan, and I want to be honest with you, so I don't think we should have sex anymore—

Aw hey, JUDY!

—for a little while, she adds, frightened into the lie.

He puts his elbows on the bar and his face in his hands, then lowers his hands, looks at her, saying, while catching the bartender's eye, and nodding for another—

Why are you killing me?

She conquers her fear, gives him a pitying look, puts her

41

hand on his arm and says,
    I'm not killing you—
    Don't you know what happened to Pollock? he asks.
    —I don't want to hurt you. I want to be your friend—I
have to go, I have to meet Kathy at the bar. Okay?
    What do you mean okay? I don't understand.
    I'd better go.
    Well maybe you'd better, though I don't know why.
    I'll call tomorrow, she says, condescending to him, yet in a
sudden awareness of her own freedom, she misses her impact
on him, which is why he as if doesn't hear her, or when she
says so long, puts the candy heart in her handbag, he says so
long too, but doesn't hear himself saying it. Before she turns to
leave, she says, guilty in her sheer relief, with a smile, however, and eyes bright—
    Come for supper tomorrow night?
    Nathan is in shock, and while he rubs his face with his
hands, and covering his eyes so as not see her, he mumbles—
    Sure, sure. . . anything. . . I don't know. . . .
    It was great, she says. But I really have to go.
    Well then, for Christ's sake go. *Really.*
    Excuse me, said a tall gaunt man in tweeds, vest, shirt,
and knit tie, I'm looking for the poet Guy Blaze.
Klatu. Not here, Blaze said.
Barrada. Never met him, mused the storyteller.
    I saw him last week in Toledo, I said, sipping my drink, in
the bus station with a bowlegged blonde. Nickto.
    Frank laughed.
    I get the message, said the stranger, and I resent it as well
as that sexist narrative I couldn't help hearing—what's your
name?
    May I rewrite that sentence? I asked.
    Kerschel 551, smiled Blaze.
    Very funny, said the tweedy man. Ha ha.

I'm angry, said the storyteller, so I'm writing angry. You creep.

The strange man muttered something from Dickens (bah), turned and left, but on the way out, gave a business card to Frank, asking if he Frank would give it to the Great Poet when next the Great Person came in. Frank thanked him, saying he would, and as the other walked out the door, Frank read the card, and with a smile walked down the duckboards to us, passed the message to Blaze who read it, and laughed, giving it to me.

You'd better wear dark glasses when you get there, I said. He's the head of the whole department, handing the card to the storyteller, who read it, and contributed—

And a false nose/mustache combo, too, and walk softly. Early in the morning.

About six weeks later.

The beginning.

From the point of view of a person walking across the Brooklyn Bridge into the city, the city stands like a sheaf of arrows to the sky, and on this particular Tuesday morning, the first Tuesday in April, and just after dawn, the sun comes up over Queens County and casts his warmth on the flanks of buildings tall enough to catch him.

The figure in this mythology, who is crossing the Bridge, is a Spirit, so it is in a sense of discovery at dawn that we follow this Spirit as it moves, in a long flowing, diaphanous robe onto the extended elegant walkway in a gradual descent where the Spirit turns north, moving ghostlike as a breeze through early morning traffic, up Centre, left on Kanal to Laughatte up which he goes to Gooper Sq, onto Fourave to Onion Park just beyond which it turns left on a crossGoof street, approaches an industrial-looking building, goes, without opening, through a heavy steel door, up a couple of flights of wide steps and at the third landing drifts through another heavy door into a very

43

large and very dark loft, where two big paintings are hung on a far wall, yet dim in the background. In spite of the darkness, it is clear the place is a mess, as is the bachelor himself who lives there, and who is at present asleep in a bed as messy as it is dirty—to which the Spirit crosses, and standing above the sleeper, speaks—

"I'm here."

Nathan wakes, and rubs his rather Oriental eyes, runs his hand through his messy white crewcut, and then across his mouth and sparse western-style mustache. He looks terrible.

He rubs his face with his hands, looks up, and after putting on round steel-rimmed glasses, rises on one elbow, and asks—

"Who are you?"

"Of your future."

"You look like it, too," Nathan smiles. "So I'm dead—and?"

"You are the painter," the figure answers. "And you are left with me."

"I get it," Nathan nods. "Dickens. It's a plot."

The Spirit seems to smile, if a warm hum can be a smile, if a hum can be warm—something from Corelli—kneels, and speaks, voice grave—

"I didn't write this script. But I know who did, and I'm giving it to you in its predicted form—tomorrow will be different."

"Different! How can anything be different! Look around you! It's hopeless!"

"True," the kneeling figure responds. "So far. But tomorrow will be different because someone will want you. You have had to suffer to receive my message—tomorrow the wheel will take another turn. Someone is approaching you. Prepare yourself."

Nathan sits up, speaking in anger—

"Me? Somebody wants *me?* Bullshit. Nobody does."

"I want you, and I say: prepare for another who likewise does."

"Why?"

"As your life will change so will mine, and tomorrow I'll want as well as need you to complete what I began."

"Yeah? I can't even paint!"

"Trust me. You'll need me, too. Here, take my hand."

Nathan puts his hand out, into a swirl of smoke, which frightens him—

"I don't understand!"

The other, yet kneeling and with soft smoke enveloping Nathan's hand, strangely glows, and soon the figure is enveloped in a radiance which suddenly begins to fade, so too the smoke, and the figure as well, but before it vanishes, its last words strike Nathan as a blow to his body—

"You weren't necessarily meant to understand, but you must know—"

Nathan pleads—"Know?"

"Yes. I'll be at your side."

The figure, fainter and fainter, seems to rise, and again, in the warm hum of Corelli, glows brilliantly, then vanishes.

Nathan bites his lip, his eyes glisten, he is as if drawn back down onto his bed, and succumbing to the force, takes off his glasses, draws the covers over himself, adjusts the pillow, and is then asleep, his spectacles in his hand, as around his head there appears a soft glow.

Softly, Blaze murmured. That's the way—may I beg one question?

Sure, the storyteller said.

You're a poet as well as a novelist—why write about a

painter?

Because nobody has, and because Hollywood and nearly everybody else around the world let Dawn Powell's novel go, we're still left with *The Horse's Mouth*, Bohemianism.

But there was the Van Gogh film, and the Gauguin—

That was biography.

True, I said, but if your Nathan is what he is or—was, I mean aren't most of those guys dead? The fifties—

Either dead or out of town, grinned the storyteller. True, but because writers, critics and the artists and others who were there when they all were alive, feared to write about them because they were alive, it is a not-so-curious paradox that because they're dead the fear is worse—look how they treat Paul Blackburn. It's as if when dead one is more feared than alive.

Yes, I said, as Blaze nodded, catching Frank's eye, but would you tell us—

We are the spirits of the dead. Their memory is in our blood, energy, vision—everything we are.

I see it! cried Blaze, red curls waving, as Frank winked at me, and made our drinks. Blaze said—Through them we can feel free to speak to, and perhaps of, ourselves.

You don't mean *just* unencumbered, I said.

No. The freedom isn't relief, it's responsibility—freedom is the discipline—death is the transfer, and if anything, in that responsibility, we're encumbered all the more, which can terrify the most astute and creative critics and writers—

Next day. Wednesday. At ten to three in the afternoon, a slender, balding, middle-aged white man in a grey gaberdine suit, red cotton shirt, pale yellow tie, black loafers and dark blue socks, walked into a bar. He went directly to the bar, not noticing two young men at one end, talking about Reggie Jackson.

The bartender was in his mid-thirties, with beard and glasses. The balding man in the gaberdine suit looked at the bartender, who was slicing pieces of peel from a lemon. Ahem, said the man in the suit. The bartender looked up, and the two stood face to face with the bar in between.

"I am looking for the painter Nathan Fierce."

"Why?" grinned the bartender, then held up his hand. "I'm only kidding. Nathan doesn't come in here anymore."

"But," said the man, "I was told this was where—"

"It was, until about six weeks ago," replied the bartender, studying the other man the way bartenders do, adding—"It's kind of personal."

"You mean not for you to say."

"You got it."

"It's personal okay," said one of the two fellows at the end of the bar, and well lemme see, okay they talk a little, the bartender and the two guys at the end, etc., and the man in the gaberdine suit says with quiet force it's urgent, in fact imperative that he see Nathan before returning to Pittsburgh on Friday.

"If you see him or can get word to him, mention I want to see his new work. My card."

Which he gives to the bartender, who glances at it, and says, aloud, The Carnegie? The two guys at the end of the bar look at each other, the one who had first spoken, in a blue sweatshirt, saying maybe Nathan can pay his bar bill, what is it, five hundred? Shut the fuck up, his friend, in bib overalls says, and okay, it goes on, they talk some more, the man from Pittsburgh saying he'd called but Nathan's telephone is disconnected, and—

Why don't you leave a note in his mailbox?" suggests the bartender.

"I didn't think of it," says the man. "But, isn't that a little old-fashioned?"

"Isn't everything?" the bartender grins.

47

Mr. Pittsburgh chuckles, thanks the bartender and well it goes on, he takes a cab to Nathan's address, leaves a note in Nathan's mail slot and continues on across town to his hotel, not noticing the pile of mail on the floor inside Nathan's front door which, as it happens, includes a bill from the gas and electric company saying if $300 and change wasn't paid in ten days, you know what. A note from his landlord, eviction in fourteen days—$1,100 etc., and the next scene is back at the bar where the three guys quarrel, the bartender upset about blue sweatshirt's mentioning Nathan's tab and maybe hurting Nathan's chance to get some good dough for a painting if that guy was a collector, knows Nathan's broke, etc., while the man from Pittsburgh tells the hotel manager he's expecting an important call, and also leaves a message at the switchboard, be sure and take the number Nathan would leave, while in another part of town Nathan—these scenes switch quickly—Nathan was sitting at the bar in a gin mill called Charley's, drinking with his friend Max, who had a thick red beard and was wearing a cowboy's Stetson, brown plaid shirt, leather vest, jeans and cowboy boots. Nathan was unshaven, his clothes rumpled and dirty. They talk and this passage is too long, and it'll need a rewrite, actually, but Nathan thanks Max for letting him spend the night with him, and apologizes for being such a bore talking about Judy and Max says look, she's only a girl and to hell with her, she's not very bright anyway, and all that talk she gave Nathan is only to sound like an adult etc., but Nathan, so distracted and depressed, only gets part of what Max says, like guys in that spot do, like I sure did, going around in circles over and over it until maybe something comes clear, and Max is getting impatient as Nathan says she loves gossip. Girls love gossip, Max says. Look, you knew it wouldn't work, and she knew she couldn't tell you the truth. See it from her point of view. Fuck her point of view, Nathan says. Well, Max says, you know what she told you — Max, speaking in that cowboy way he has, says she drawing out the e, she wanted, drawing out the a: d, venture, and though I know it hurts your feelings old buddy, but she doesn't want anybody in her way, you most of all. Yeah, Nathan agrees, I guess she had to get rid of me. Right, Max says, but, Nathan says, she also said which I've told you — yes, Max says, you have — she wants, Nathan says anyway, she wants to be friends which means Max says as I've told you (Nathan doesn't remember), she wants to use you as a so-called friend. Look what you did for her! Do you think she wants to let that go? She said, Nathan says, she wished I was ten years younger or she was ten years older, and Max sighs, says she's just a girl. She'll go home for Thanksgiving, eat turkey with Mom Dad Sis and Junior and give dark meat to the dog, have a shot of creme de menthe afterwards and go for a walk with Dad and three days later will be back in town without having thought of you once, she's a girlll you know girlllls, they know tact like horses know Latin. Listen, Nathan asks, do you have any money? Max puts ten on the bar and says Nathan, come with me. You're free! Come to Taos! Sell your loft, you'll get a fortune for that place, get somebody to keep your paintings and get out of this goofy city, that sure sounds good, Nathan says, cheered a little, well, Max says, if it sounds *good, do* it, let's gee oh GO! let's get you a *woman*, you're a *man*, you need a *woman*, not a *girlll*, you're too — aw what the hell's the word, dedicated? for a girl, you're too — whatever anybody wants to call it, important? Not important enough for Alice, Nathan says, well Max says you sure blew that one, but Nathan I'm tellin' ya, you know yourself, you have this illusion of yourself, you Goddamned romantic, that's true, Nathan says, I do, you're right, but it's impossible, Alice was *always* right, she made me so Goddamned guilty and well, well I got Goddamned sick of it and her and there's a flashback —

49

He breathed, sipped his drink, lit a smoke, had another
sip, and said Nathan was drunk, smashed and angry, staggering around the loft waving his arms, as he occasionally turns,
and though unsteadily, faces Alice who is also angry, as he
yells—You're *always* right and I'm ALWAYS *wrong. You*
don't get drunk, you don't forget anything, you get it all—
everything figured out BAM—you're a *good person*—you,
Alice says, wouldn't say this if you were sober and he says I
wouldn't say a lot of things and you wouldn't say that if you
were drunk, I DON'T she yells GIVE A DAMN! I DON'T
WANT TO HEAR ANY MORE WHEN YOU'RE DRUNK
YOU ARE IM *POSSIBLE!* Okay yeah unh huh and, he
says, pointing at her, it's the same when I'm sober *don't lie to
me,* advancing on her making a fist, don't *lie* to me! and she
backs away, angry but frightened, and yet defiant, you
wouldn't *dare* hit me! I want to, he says, and one of these
days I'm going to start saying things when I'm sober, I'm
angry enough and—as a matter of fact ADMIT you hate me,
and *you* said it, not me, it was you who said you hated me
when my ego was rewarded and you were jealous. Do you
think that makes me happy?—made me happy? With every
success I got, I got your jealousy? True, she admits, and I'm
sorry your sales are down, and it is as if they are each other's
voices of reason and unreason, yes, it's true, and I admit it,
I'm a bitch that way, but we can work that out—I will, I'll try,
but then she's angry, then very angry, saying but that doesn't
give you—no, that isn't why you're drinking so much—do
you know why? No, he says, yes, sure, I'm fucked up, and
she says you want *everything the way you want it* and when
you get it you're guilty because you wanted it that way, but
when you don't have it that way you're furious, and guilty for
being so furious. Why aren't you angry at your Mother—she
started it, that illusion, because her illusion was that you
could have it your way OH NO he yells, it wasn't an illusion,

it was her wish! All right, Alice cries, but you MADE IT AN ILLUSION, you're right, Nathan says, turning red in the face, and I'm wrong again. You, she says, you self-pitying bastard, I ought to kill you he says, don't you think *I'm* not angry at *her?* or that I don't envy your success? Do you think—think how I feel, he continues, when I come home to your success: You're getting the good reviews, not me, and—DO YOU, she shrieks—DO YOU THINK I WANT TO COME HOME TO *YOU?* as two small children sit up in their beds, in a far corner of the loft, and watch, lips tight, and eyes wide, sadly. Nathan looked at Max, and perspiring in the sudden memory said, I can't paint and I must have scared hell out of Judy.

Judy and Nathan reach the top step in front of the door to her loft, and because he is so drunk he staggers backwards, reaches for the railing, misses, and before she can catch him, he falls head over heels down the flight of stairs. She rushes down to him, but he lies still, and taking his head in her hands, asks, in terror—

Nathan—hey, Nathan, are you okay?

He sits up, himself frightened, and rubbing his head, says, dazed, Yeah, what the hell happened?

She gapes, not sure what to say, and shaken by his loss of memory—

You fell down the steps!

Then, as she helps him up the stairs, she says, in a plea—Listen Nathan, you—you ought to quit drinking, I mean a—little.

Maybe she was so afraid of me she manipulated it, Nathan said. Max shrugged his shoulders and said at that point you didn't give her much else, adding, women can do that. You know. Women hate drunks.

You said Judy was a girl.

They're all women, Max said, they're born women, and

51

somewhere along the line too many turn into girls and it begins all over again different.

They're clever, you know. Not like us.

You want me to agree?

They're cruel, too.

So are we, Max said, and sighed, saying look old buddy, look what you gave her, so no matter what else, she got used to you, and whenever she needed Daddy to smooth things out, she came to you, annnnd youuuuu smooooothed things out! Okay, she got used to it, which is why she'll miss you—my tenses are wrong—which is why she missed you until she didn't.

Which was why she slept with me.

Not at first, Max said, in wisdom adding, at first she liked you very much, and it was fun. Then she learned. It wasn't you—it was any man. Let her go, my old Nathaniel Love. Let her go her adventurous ways. Why not? Let her have your bar, it's a hopeless place anyway, and let 'em gossip. They're bored, unimaginative and so self-involved you don't exist. You're better than any of 'em—come, Max pointed to his chest and leaned close, saying, voice gentle, in Nathan's ear: Come west with me.

Nathan grinned as he wiped a tear from his eye. Max put his arm around Nathan's shoulder. His voice was tender.

Don't worry about being impotent. You'll get over it. It's happened to me—to a lot of men. One day you'll be some place some where and your eyes will run into another pair of eyes, you'll know, and the rest will be history. Meanwhile, pour it, pour all of it into your work.

That's good, Nathan said. Thanks. I—I have to go up and see Alice and the kids this evening, but first I want to take a nap, and clean up. Can you let me have twenty? Max gave him another ten, saying he too had a date, but why not have one for the road, which they did, and after they had parted on the sidewalk, Nathan walked home, picked up his mail without looking at it, knowing what it was, and so depressed when he got into his loft he threw the pile onto another pile of un-opened mail, and yawning, crossed his loft, but stopped in his tracks—a figure was on his bed! No, it was only the blankets and sheets twisted into the shape, and as he took off his clothes and got into bed, he set the cheap windup clock and put his head down, but—sat up thinking he had seen someone—or something, right by the bed! A glow! But—what, was it a dream? Yet then he was asleep, and across the city Judy walked out onto the sidewalk from the ad agency where she worked, caught a bus downtown, got off, walked to her loft building, went inside, up the stairs and into her loft where she made herself a cup of tea, lit a smoke, set the alarm, took off all her clothes and stretched out naked on her bed, drinking tea, smoking, and gazing at the ceiling.

Her good sized loft was in the mess of a farm girl alone in the city. Her paintings, finished and unfinished, hung on walls and lay spread out on the floor. A full human skeleton hung from a hook atop a vertical rod fixed on a pedestal beside her painting wall which was across the loft from her bed and closet. Seen closeup, sections of the skeleton were seen in her paintings, in particular the hip bone.

She put out the cigarette, and took a nap, woke, put on her paint clothes and began to consider a large unfinished painting, which had to its left, also stapled to the wall, a blank canvas the same size as the one she was considering, in fact she was considering both of them.

Nathan stands beside her as she sits in a chair facing the painting on the wall, and he is saying she has to discipline and extend her thought process, and she says she doesn't know how to think. It isn't, he says, your fault, nobody can be taught to think—most schools don't do that, but don't put a dot on that new canvas until you know how and where and with what color you want to begin.

But how will I know? she cries.

Well, DeKooning said he knows when a painting is done because it tells him, so if we can listen to that tip, which it is, we can watch until it begins. It's there—he points to the blank canvas—it's right there, and you have to find it. Keep looking.

She makes a sad face, and with a rather forlorn gaze up at Nathan, says that's okay for DeKooning, but how about me?

Look at it until you know, and *don't* be impulsive. But Judy shakes her head, and bites her lip as Nathan says well, then work on something else—do some drawings. Get involved with something so you'll see this with a fresh eye.

Judy chewed on the nail of her left index finger, went to her paint table which was a mess, squeezed cadmium red medium onto an almost paint-covered sheet of glass, rubbed a brush in a can of turpentine, and then into the paint and with brush in hand walked to the blank canvas, and just before she began the stroke, she heard Nathan say—"*don't* be impulsive"—so she lowered the brush and stood there, then spoke aloud to herself—I don't know what in the HELL I'm *doing!*

Look, Nathan says, look until you see something—a form or color that looks like it belongs there, and think about as well as visualize where that form or color can go—can a vertical stroke indicate a horizontal—or vice versa?

But, she says, I know how to look, and he realizes she's making gestures like him, and as he listens, she's imitating his speech, too!—but I don't know how to think while I'm looking!

Nathan is tender. I know, he says, try—work at extending your concentration, your visual attention span, you'll have to, keep looking, exploring, look until you're so far into it all you can see is the structure—gesturing to the skeleton—let the Professor of Art History at The University of Nowhere, Class of '86, may he rest in peace—help you. There's structure, and a lot of painting's like that, as organic as a body, so when you're inside your structure, look around at what's there until you can arrange it with your eye and your visual memory using your mind as the connection.

But that's you talking about your painting, she says.

That's true, he agrees, but being inside a painting and looking around it is universal, so is visual thinking. It doesn't just happen, bingo a picture. Images, lines, forms, color all have their connection and action, whether it's Albers or Michaelangelo.

She slumps back in her chair, stares at the floor, folds her hands in her lap and whispers I know, Goddammit! bitterly, she said, standing up.

She crossed to the other painting, the unfinished one next to the skeleton, and looked at the white patch in the upper right hand corner, intently: This, Nathan says, gesturing to that patch, is what can happen when you're not concentrating.

Overpaint, she says.

You said it. He gestures to a red area in the left center, saying this is what you can do when you're in it. You're a damned good painter, so you can do it. This red over this red over this ochre transparency lets the paint through, and this, gesturing to the white patch, is the coverup white on the kitchen wall, letting nothing through, and she says you mean it's just blah bloppo, and then nods, eyes bright, That's good! Let it come through! Thanks!

I want to go into this detail, the storyteller said, because in books or in print anywhere, and most of all in film, it's just never done, never of contemporary painting—or music—think of a movie where Bird, or Diz or Miles eat, sleep, walk, practice, see people, argue, arrange, compose, worry—and play, consider the *hard* work they do!

I murmured assent which Blaze in his style echoed, and

the three of us smiled in each's own marvelous vision of a fictional movie on jazz that could bring a veracity nobody's ever seen . . . we sipped our handsome drinks. She scratched her head, returned to her chair, sat down and looked at the blank canvas. Her eyes were in slits as she puffed on her cigarette, and in a quick motion, rose to her feet, ground out the butt on the floor, moved to the canvas—her hands were empty as she had put the brush on her palette—and as she pointed to a place just left of center, she said—If I put the red here, which is what I want to do, where will I put the ochre—here? she gestured just to the right, but, *if* I do, what will that do? No, too enclosed, maybe change brushes? Nathan said vary the brush strokes—she backed away, face beginning to intensify and brighten, and while looking at the blank canvas, with steady, almost hard eyes, she went to the stove, lit the burner under the kettle glancing at the canvas, took a tea bag out of a box, glancing at the canvas, put the bag in an empty cup, and as the water heated she looked at the canvas.

She walked to the chair with the cup of hot tea, and sat down, sipping and looking at the canvas. She put the cup on the floor, rose, crossed to her paint table, picked up the brush with the red paint on it, ran it once twice in the paint again, went to the canvas, took a deep breath, and with a light motion, scrubbed a wobbly vertical line, stepped back, went to her paint table, squeezed yellow ochre onto the glass, selected a three-inch brush from a coffee can of brushes, smeared it in turps and in ochre paint, and in a rapid move to the canvas she made a broad, and again wobbly, stroke across the top of the red, stepped back, looked at it, sat in the chair brush in hand, sipped tea, and said great.

"What next?"

She rose, went to the rather ancient refrigerator, took out a lemon and as she sliced it in two she glanced at her new beginning, and as if in intuition glanced at the wall above the sink where a small framed drawing of her hung neatly between her mirror and a drinking glass of daisies, with Nathan's pencilled message in the lower right hand corner of the drawing—*To Judy with Love*—NF, and the date, and to the other side of the mirror at a framed photo of him, standing before a huge, almost mural-sized finished canvas in brilliant colors. He was in his paint clothes, wide brush in hand, and not quite smiling, his head tilted to the right. She glanced at her fresh work, sucked on the lemon. Blue? she said to the painting, and crossing the floor sat down in the chair, lemon half in hand. Let's not kid ourselves, she said. What I want is a drink! Fuck this art stuff! Sighing deeply, Nathan is sitting beside her at the bar. It is the first week of the New Year. Her arm is over his shoulder, and her face is concerned as he says in anger, Yeah. But when *I* say fuck this art stuff, that means I'm hot and can afford it—comic luxury. But I'm *not* hot, I can't walk away from it like you. You can because you're working, and can come back to it and I can't work at all which means I've got nothing to come back to—remember, I have a show this fall— the end of September is tomorrow to me, and Goddammit Judy, I sat in front of that blank canvas for six hours today. It's been like this for weeks. Something is *all* wrong. Alice is going crazy, the kids are upset and I can't seem to connect with it—it's in there, I *know* it is, right *in* there, and I can't—it won't let me in—he sighs, rubs his his forehead and mutters I'm impossible, I know, I know.

No, she says, you're not impossible, you're great, and you're in a damned difficult situation—yet there's an edge in her voice that she can't control, above a voice that seems to want to push through, which would change or rearrange the sentences, and the voice he would then have heard would have been something different—a slight cruelty slightly. She rose, put both brushes in the turps, put the rest of the lemon back in the fridge, washed up looking in the mirror, dried off, put on clean clothes, her raincoat and hat, and left, locking the door behind her, and on the first turn of the second landing, she stopped, and—stared ahead.

Rose red!

Turned, and taking two steps each jump, returned to her loft murmuring then ochre again, almost running to her paint table, coattails flying she squeezed rose red onto the glass, cleaned a brush, pushed it into the paint, ran it back and forth, crossed to the new painting, and with wide, bright, intense eyes said, Yes, right there, and then ochre to the right—firmly, walking along Vantyir St. with Nathan. He is holding her right hand with his left hand and is vivid, gesturing with his right hand in obvious exhilaration as Judy listens, her face radiant and eyes intent as he says—

It's utterly *wild* how it suddenly unfolds—and falls into place! It's like Cecil Taylor! Alice says novels work like that too—the whole Goddammed thing! BAM like *that*, he snaps his fingers—and laughs, tossing his head madly, Judy stepped to the painting, and with a grim smile, said BAM, snapped her fingers to the painting—like *that*, applied rose red, stepping back nimbly as Nathan stepped out of an elevator, walked along a carpeted hallway and stopped before a door, pushed the button, heard muted chimes, and stood in thought until the door opened and Alice was before him. They looked at each other.

Whereas Judy was pretty in a plain, youthful sense, Alice was an adult east coast knockout. She was thirty-five. Her skin was flawless, her body was solid, and supple. She had beautiful legs, and slender ankles. Tonight, however, she looked tired, and neither she nor Nathan spoke as he entered the apartment. After she had closed the door, they stood, looking at each other.

"Hi," she said, in soft voice. "How are you."

58

"I'm okay," he smiled. "How are you?"

"I'm okay," she shrugged. "Things are tough. You know."

He nodded. "I know."

He glanced through the narrow foyer into the living room, and saw her desk. His eyes were almost longing. He loved her involvement with her art. She said—

"Are you painting."

"No, and I'm still fucked up. Arthur called from the gallery the day before my phone was cut off, and said he was enthusiastic about things. I lied to him, saying I was too and that I was working well."

"You should lie to him," Alice said. "When is the show? September? I'm so tired I can't remember. Sorry."

"Don't be sorry," Nathan said, his voice gloomy, "it's the end of September. Where are the kids? In bed?"

"You're almost two hours late—Matt's getting over a sinus attack and Sally's got a cold. Yes, they're in bed."

"I took a nap," he said, making a face. "I overslept. That cheap ass clock I bought doesn't always work."

They went into the living room, and sat on the sofa.

Her apartment was alive with color and warmth, although it was, in design, routine, and too expensive. Yet her plants by the front windows—view south—and her good collection of good books filled bookcases, which having been made to order—the bookcases—gave the room a handsome professional character, and a feel of sensibility, education and thought. Her records filled a cabinet built like her bookcases, on top of which was her stereo system—she had excellent taste in music, so her records were marvelous, and unless you liked details, you might—for the plants, pictures and furniture around—miss the classy seven-foot long modern desk, with her electric typewriter on it, beside which was a ream of white paper, a box of carbon paper, and one of second sheet onionskin, and to the right of the typewriter, the first draft of a new novel in a box next to and just in front of a Mason jar of jonquils, behind which, in lean-to frames, were colored photos of the kids in Paris, and Rome, as if they and the jonquils were (which was true) her inspiration to the completed draft before them. The kids had big grins in the photos, and why not? Wouldn't you like a lemonade on the Champs Elysées?

On the wall above her desk was a framed, and inscribed to her, drawing by Philip Guston, and beside it the framed note from Doris Lessing telling Alice that her first novel revealed a clear and vital feminine voice.

A large fern hung from the ceiling, as a plumb line, above her typewriter.

Nathan was jealous.

"Well," she smiled, "this has happened before. Remember that show you did in two weeks?"

They laughed.

"So," she went on, "you've got a little more than four-and-a-half months. You can do it."

"Yes," he agreed. "I know. But they're—each show is different—you know—and I'm—blank. I can't see a thing. Anything."

"Are you still seeing Judy?"

"No. I've—made up my mind. She wants—" Nathan sighed—"to be friends."

Alice made a solemn nod. "It seems to me I've heard that song before. What are you going to do?"

"I don't know. I might sell the loft and go west with Max. He asked me today . . . but—I don't know."

She cleared her throat and looked at him. She looked at him. She said that was madness, and, after a pause which embarrassed him, said, in a voice to split shotputs, he could at least sublet, before he ran away. "Again," she added, and he bit his lip in guilt.

"Are you still drinking?"

He nodded as she looked at him, but avoided her eyes. She said,

"I want to tell you something. Which fell into place today. When you introduced me to Judy—" speaking almost casually.

Nathan and Judy are walking east on a street midGoof, when Nathan spots Alice and her friend Charlene coming toward them.

"Oh oh," he says.

"What's the matter?" Judy asks.

"There's Alice, and her pal Charlene."

Judy turns pale, shows fright and dismay. "What shall I—"

"I'll handle it for Christ's sake," he says. "Don't worry."

"Don't worry he says," she says.

The two couples meet, and Nathan smiles to Alice.

"Hi sweetheart," and says hi to Charlene, who looks at Judy, Alice looks at Judy, who looks at the sidewalk. Alice and Charlene look at Nathan, who looks back at them. "Alice—and Charlene—this is my friend Judy," he says. Alice and Charlene say hello. Judy mumbles,—a mumble. Alice, with a cool city smile, says, to Nathan, like bad teeth hitting the pit in the peach—

"It's nice to meet you Judy. I'll see you later, Nathan. Did you remember to take the veal out of the freezer?"

"Right. The brussel sprouts too."

"Fine," Alice says, and the couples part, but while Alice and Charlene stand on the corner, waiting for the light to change, Alice frowns, and murmurs,

"She reminds me of someone. Who—who—I wonder . . ."

"Another Agatha Christie mystery?" Charlene grins, and they laugh, linking arms.

"She reminded me of someone, and until today I couldn't remember who."

Alice paused, looking at Nathan, as he sat beside her, looking at the opposite wall like painters look at opposite walls. Like men do.

He looked at her.

"She reminded me of your sister, and you will remember that you told me, when you quit therapy, that Dr. Hartman, in speaking of your mother brought up the subject of your sister, saying, in fact, which you don't remember, because you were so smashed when you told me, that *your sister had in fact been your mother*. You also don't remember a couple of other things—let me finish—first, in your cracked associative process, you joked about her as in Rider Haggard's *She*—'Who Must Be Obeyed'—and, that for some reason you quote couldn't figure out unquote you thought of your sister, which, it turns out, was just after you'd met Judy."

"You've been busy," he said.

"I've been busy," she replied. "Nathan—Nathan look, if you try and keep this going on with her—she's used you to her satisfaction, she doesn't need or want you anymore. She gained a giant step into the art world through the door which you opened for her, and she's young, clever, and ambitious. You're in her way. And—you're too old not to know what's going to happen. You can't lean on her like you did on me. She's going to want—which she will get—her independence."

"I'm through with her! She's got it! Alice! Lay off!"

"But if I don't tell you, who will? The boys at the bar? Or Max? You know how he resists therapy—and while you're moping around town feeling sorry for yourself, you're talking to anybody—bartenders, waitresses—anybody who will listen! Do you think they care? Do you believe anyone cares as I do? Why don't you call Dr. Hartmann—find out what in hell is going on in you—"

"Nobody gives a damn except you,"—angry—"and I know it, as well as I know, yes, I should call him. You're right.

Again."

She put her hand on his leg, and shifted position so as she sat she was looking square in his face.

"I'm not going to worry about you. I can't."

"I know. I'm worried about you too. And the kids."

"They miss you—you *must* take care of yourself—and those skyrocketing *bar*tabs."

"I will, I—am, I will, don't worry, please."

"I can't," she said, voice grim. "Have you told your mother about us?"

"No. I can't."

"There's the phone," Alice pointed.

"I—can't from here. I'll use Max's."

"That might be better. Promise?"

"Promise."

"You've broken a lot of those. You've also lied."

He hung his head—"You're hitting hard, Alice—hard, and quick."

"I've been thinking," she replied, in a calm tone. "I'm hitting hard—hard and quick? I almost cracked up after I left the courthouse that day. You know. And when I phoned you to tell you divorce proceedings had been finalized—I'd told you I would phone—you said, and this was all you said, you said you knew I was upset and you began talking about your not being able to paint and the gallery. To give my bat a more gentle swing, that wasn't very considerate. I was a great deal more than upset. I had to go—from the courthouse—to that God-damned job, and when I got there I closed the door to my office, and—" she lowered her head and wept. "Nathan, I wept all afternoon."

He put his arm around her, her head went on his shoulder as he said, with tears in his eyes, while kissing the top of her head—

"I know. Jesus I hated myself."

He caressed her cheek. She moved away and looked at him as she wiped her eyes. —

"All this because of you." She sniffled. "You know I love you."

"I still love you."

"You were so wonderful, and such a bastard, such a baby. Please call Dr. Hartmann."

"I will."

"Promise?"

"Alice, I promise."

"Nathan—don't break *this* one."

"Alice," he growled, "I—PROMISE!" he yelled, and a ten-year-old boy came into the room, and seeing Nathan, smiled, sleepy-eyed.

"Hi Daddy, Mommy can I have some orange juice?"

"Sure," she said, getting up, and as she went into the kitchen, the boy went to Nathan, who held out his hands and the boy let his body be taken in his father's embrace. Daddy, he said—

"I miss you. Can I visit you?"

Nathan, visualizing the mess his loft was in, said sure, "but I got to get that place cleaned up! It's a wreck."

"A wreck," the boy repeated, laughing, and rubbing sleep from his eyes. "A *fuckin'* wreck?"

"A *fuckin'* wreck," Nathan laughed. They laughed together as the boy sat beside Nathan, who asked,

"How's school?"

"Hopeless," the boy grinned, but Nathan's face had changed and gone through the several colors of feeling into the memory-realization that he might leave town.

"Listen, Matt I forgot, I—I might be leaving town for a couple of months, but I—I'll be back for my—show oh shit what will I *do?* I'll do some watercolors out there, Goddamned Arthur likes small stuff—"

But Matt was looking at his father in anger, and when Alice came back with the glass of juice, which she handed to Matt, she said, in anger, to Nathan—

"Can't you talk to your son without talking about yourself?"

"Maybe, just maybe not," he said.

Matt drank the juice, watching them.

"You're impossible," she said.

"That's possible, but you aren't."

"Both of you are," Matt said, and Nathan and Alice laughed—once, stopped, and looked at each other in a silent bitterness.

"Did you write this script?" Nathan asked her.

"No, did you?"

"Not me, you're the writer."

She gave him a look, and he held up his hands, in apology as he apologized sorry—sorry sorry.

Matt put the empty glass on the coffee table in front of the sofa, slipped down off, and with his head down, left the room.

Alice, in restrained fury, said "I can't believe it."

Her face went pale, and a thin white crescent appeared at each end of her lips. Her words were just audible.

" Do not wise crack about scripts treat me as I *am* and *not* as you do your MOTHER!"

"I'm sorry!" he cried. "Alice! I'm sorry!"

"But it's that sarcasm of yours again—did you see Matt's face as he left? Did you Nathan? Isn't it a little late for apologies? Do you know what you do? No. You don't know what you do—to me as well, and yes, you are sorry, of course you're sorry, what dimwit like you wouldn't be sorry, and meanwhile you're hostile. I know you're angry at me, but don't confuse Matt and Sally with those hostile wisecracks— save 'em for the boys at the bar they'll love 'em, Nathan! Grow up! Act your age!"

"Painters are hopeless including me. I'm hopeless I know, and if you think he can't hear you in there, you're mistaken. You're not helping any."

"I'll take that risk," she snapped—" I've been thinking about us, going over and over it until I come to something, and—because I am so Goddamned *angry* I can not suppress it and if it confuses him, I'll accept the blame, but as compulsive as I am about order and neurotic about my father I feel my anger is real."

She stood, hands in fists, looking down at him—

"In reality, you fool, you are not hopeless. You know you're the best, and yes—things are tough for you, but isn't that one test of your force, your strength and skill in terms of your commitment, and your integrity? You wouldn't think to compromise your integrity because it wouldn't occur to you —you're *the* painter, you're not another one, and can't you try and be that as a man as well? You have so much, *so much,* remember what Sir Herbert Read said of your work? *He saw you* Nathan—you *have so much and you're so horrible."*

She sat down beside him, took his hand, and looking at him—

"Nathan I don't want to fight, but—you see I I don't know what to do with my anger. You kept me waiting for two hours, that old trick of yours, but I know—Nathan be honest with me. I know you don't want to see me or be with me, which is why I divorced you. I know you're afraid of me, and though I think I know why, and therefore understand, I I mean, to—what do we do when we know the truth?"

Nathan was watching her, and his eyes were careful.

She was in thought.

"Truth is tricky," she murmured. "In our case volatile. For example, if I would mention a truth which you know is true, I would be telling a truth, in a sense, of a truth, which is

more than redundant because the knowledge of the case over-
comes the truth wanting to be stated, as you know enough
about women to know it is true women have contempt for men
who fear them, and I must, in order to clear my mind, tell you
that as a woman I have contempt for you—as well as for the
women who use that fear to manipulate the men who feel it.
They're the worst of all."

"The women."

"The women. I've a lot of criticism of men, I've been hard
at work as of late, but there's plenty left for the ladies."

"But not as much as for the men."

"No, not as much."

"And different."

"Yes. Different."

"What do you think it is—you just said—"

"I think," she said, frowning in concentration, an expression, a look that warmed his heart, and caused a certain smile.

Because she was so deep in thought she—she knew him—
she overlooked the warmth she knew he was feeling, but in the
beginning she had asked him, and his honest reply had, in this
one sense, caused her to trust him. In that respect. The other
respect was when he was painting and himself in thought. Her
heart had warmed too. The third, and last trust, was rare, but
memorable, for when he was happy with himself, and in a real
sense, loved himself, she was head-over-heels in love with
him, although, it was true, she was jealous. It was hard if not
impossible that there could be anyone who could be so wonderful, so much fun, so giving, and so profound—in the flesh!
Who, she had often considered, wouldn't be jealous. But after
that, things became very very complicated, as Nathan's hatred
of himself, his terrible self-destructive streaks, his almost
overwhelming guilt—and when he wasn't painting, he was
impossible, yet, she also knew, in that follow-up way, so was

she, and when they both weren't working, her control in-furiated him as his out-of-control lunacy infuriated her, and this, which she likewise knew—she was smarter than Nathan—made her a little guilty, for in a way she would never speak, she envied his madness (he didn't know that), and in a dark little corner way back in her mind and heart, she hated him with a ferocity she dared not admit, for though she was smarter than Nathan, he was brilliant beyond words, and unwilling to admit her limitation, in her unconscious she would have given her life for it, thus, in this baffling truth, she was divided in a way most unusual, and most difficult to handle, and in a way toward a touch of it, she admitted the case as the case being as the case was, yet, it could be considered a miracle they had come this far, for excellence living with greatness was, to be sensible, at least a farfetched notion, Why, she wondered, why was she *so* angry at herself?

She rose, crossed to her desk, and made a notation on a piece of paper—

It isn't all Nathan, it's me too. Feel divided in anger, vindictive, bitchy—call Dr. Z.

Nathan was having difficulty himself, for seeing her in a rather new light, he saw how incredibly beautiful she was, and what a fool he had been, but—it came as a shock to him—beauty could be a fateful trick, to blind the eye of the beholder, and—in his follow-up way—he realized he wasn't afraid of her, never had been, but he was *in awe of her*, and as he wasn't as introspective as Alice, nor could he sustain his introspection as she, it stopped, and he felt good, albeit a little curious, yet he felt a gentle, very gentle prod within that told him while he loved her, true, in actuality he also did not very much like her, and, though she loved him, it was quite possible she hated him and—herself! no, couldn't be true. But she was speaking.

"Wait," he said. "I was thinking—realizing something, and missed the first part."

"What did you realize?"

"A lot. I'm not—as we thought—afraid of you. I'm in awe."

"You're in awe of all women."

"I know what you're thinking," he said, "because I know you, although I don't know all you think. But in that last blanket statement, you are wrong, as for example I am not in awe of Judy."

"True," she admitted. "I went too far, but—"

"Wait, let me finish—I admit, it's true, I can fear some of the things women can feel—the things that characterize women. You're not going to tell me you don't fear certain things about me—"

His voice was sarcastic, he had a wry smile.

She made a parallel smile, but her eyes had a gleam of triumph. She said that was good—

"You are intuitive, Nathan. That's pretty close to what I was just saying—if your mother had shown her anger, or rage, at you, you wouldn't fear me or any woman."

Her smile faded, and her face became grim.

"You fear women's anger, don't you."

"Not with a quart of vodka in me."

She moved her head a little, said oh a funny man ha ha and looked at him. "Shall I?" she asked herself. "Yes," she answered.

"All right," voice firm, she began. "You, in your actual sense, fear me—my anger—because you fear your own anger, which is why you drink, to control your anger, and your guilt, until you get so drunk the anger comes out, but I know you, and you've changed. I'll admit I have problems myself, along these lines, and I'm working with them, hard as I can, but we're very different people. For example, which is not true of me, your honest—or whatever they call it—self, isn't satisfied with drinking, I mean just drinking, because it—that self—wants answers, solutions, or a way into or out of things, problems, etc., and in an actual sense, you use it, you use your drinking to find out how you feel, how to react, respond, often what to say, and because most often you're angry, you've grown in the sense that you've found out how angry you are, why you are angry and—to a point, how to handle it, but, which you know, you need to know more, so—yet what's clear to me," she continued, crossing her legs and turning to face him, pointing her self at him, "when you don't fear me you're too angry to fear—with that quart of vodka in you—and as you don't bluff your anger—you're good that way, and I might, I—Jesus, do I envy that? Hm, there's a thought, anyway, you're honest, and I'm convinced that conscious or not you know that the way to me is, in this strange logic, through anger *but* it's difficult for you—not so much as it used to be—to express that anger when you're sober, although you feel it. Are you sober?"

"Yes, and I'm angry at you."

"Good. Not long ago you wouldn't have said either. But I'm sure you want a drink, right?"

"Right. How's your new novel coming?"

"First draft done, and corrected. I'll begin typing the final tomorrow."

"Do you like it?"

"Love it," she smiled.

Jesus, he thought—how beautiful she is!

"You're beautiful," he said. "What an asshole I was."

"Right on both points," she replied. "My agent waits, so she tells me, on pins and needles for it. A curious cliché for a literary agent, no?"

"If they're as blockheaded as gallery people, it isn't," he smiled.

They both smiled.

"I have to give it to my former publisher so they'll reject it and lose their option."

"But why? I know they were miserable to you, but—"

"My agent met an editor at Viking at a party last week who likes my work *very* much, and who is *very* eager to meet me, and very much *more* wants to see the new novel."

"More money. I get it—good luck sweetheart! Say—what did you do with that story about Sally?"

"Well, my agent says she's sure *The Atlantic* will take it. It's in the hands of the final editor, and the other editors want it."

"Terrific. What will you do?"

"With the money if they take it, and *if* Viking takes my book, and through my agent I'll get a better advance, and higher royalty rates than if I met the editor and handled it myself— anyway, I'll spend August on Nantucket, and God willing, the next two months in the south of France."

"With the kids?"

"With the kids."

"And school?"

"I don't know, don't care, and am not thinking about it, but one thing is clear, though I like this apartment and can work here, it's very expensive. I've got a little over a thousand in the bank, so everything is if if if. I don't know. Dad says he'll help, but that's the last resort."

"That creep. But you have your job—"

"Yes, and I have Matt and Sally too."

"Yeah—Jesus Alice, you're great. You're wonderful, beautiful, one hell of a good writer, and an all around miracle tough as gristle."

"Don't go overboard, I'm not so tough. I can take care of the kids all right, but it would help—them as well as me—if you could take them more often." She paused. "Take care of yourself, Nathan. They need you. Straighten out."

"Okay, I—will. I'll call Hartmann, I promise—I want to. I'll explain to Max I have to have a couple of weeks.

"A couple of weeks," she said. "A couple of weeks won't help, you know that, but—" she struggled— "oh, maybe something—will, I don't know—happen in a different way, to—I—oh hell, I don't know. Oh Nathan! Is there—I'm very tired. Is there something on tv? Look and see, would you?"

"Let's pretend," he smiled.

She began to smile, but anger crossed her face. He got an oh-oh look that meant those wisecracks again, hearing her say yes, those wisecracks again. But.

"Maybe we should," she joked, rising and crossing the room to the television set, from off of which she took the TV Guide, and returned to sit by Nathan, and as he put his arm around her she snuggled in, and they looked through the listings together.

"Doesn't look good," he said.

"We missed M*A*S*H," she murmured. "And Nova, dammit."

"Listen," he said. "I'm starved. Are there any leftovers?"

"Sure," she answered, and they rose, went into the kitchen, and as he sat at a small table she opened the refrigerator and took out meat, mustard, put it on a plate which she handed him with a knife, fork and paper napkin. As he ate, she made a little salad and joined him.

"How are Jake and Arlene?"

"Fine."

"I'm glad you're working well. In fact I'm jealous." He laughed.

"You, jealous?" she laughed. "But, yes, I'm glad too. Look Nathan, once you get busy, you'll be happy again, not jealous. You know that. But—are you—are you serious about going west? I can't believe you'd sell the loft—"

"Well Goddammit," he said, "I don't know. But I'm getting nothing nada and zilch done here, so maybe I will—I don't know. Big Dom who owns that bar has wanted it for years, as you know, and as he needs big space to paint in—I—well he has a lot of money, and at this point I'm so desperate—"

"But you'd come back here with no place to work!"

"Yeah, that's a little problem I don't want to think about. Can you imagine it? Me back in town and no loft, but if I do okay on my show, I'll be able to get a new place, and—"

"Nathan," she interrupted, "be realistic. You're very deep in debt. Your sales are down. Don't grab at straws—"

"Or swizzlesticks. I know, you're right. But—well, I have the two big ones done and they're the best yet. They'll be the foundation for the show. Everything else goes around them. Do you have any wine?"

She rose, went to the cupboard, and returned with a bottle of red, and two glasses which she filled saying she was forgetting the obvious these days.

"Me too," he agreed, drinking. "Are you working on anything else?"

"A book, novel maybe, of interwoven stories—about us."

He lowered the glass, pointed to her, and then at himself. "Us?"

"Worried?" she smiled, sipping.

"I'm not worried," he said, on the defense.

She put her glass on the table, and looked at him.

"There," she said, "you go again."

"What does that mean?" he cried. "I said I wasn't worried! I trust you!"

"Why aren't you worried? I would be. You're not worried about what I think is true? It's good you're a painter! Don't you know that I'm in awe of you, and your truth? And don't you know—you said it, not me—that you frighten me too?"

"Well, yeah—sure, I—mean, I aw hell Alice look, I know your writing, and you wouldn't—"

"*Wouldn't I?*"

His face fell, and his eyes showed alarm, fear, and guilt. "Yeah," he muttered. "I guess you would."

"That's what I meant when I said I was thinking about us, in part anyway, because I was, to be honest, thinking of us yes, but of my new book, too. Some things are coming clear. I'll miss you Nathan, but there's a lot of you I won't."

"Ditto here."

"Ditto there? You're a writer's dream. What do you think it was like—listen, if you think it was any fun listening to you talk about that manipulating bitch Judy, you're mistaken. I've never seen you so stupid. I don't know why I didn't *demand* you to see Hartmann, but it was probably because I was so confused—concerned and shook up I wasn't thinking straight. You behaved—to be generous, although I don't know why I should be generous—you behaved like a child, and I let myself mother you. I want to write about that. I want to write about that so it burns, so when I hit those keys the paper will scream, I'm telling you, you came to me, and—"

"I know what I did—for Christ's sake!"

"But you didn't know how I felt! Nathan! You used me, you terrified me, drunk and crying and raving—how do you think *I* felt, God knows I knew what *you* felt, and God and myself together know, as sure as Heaven above, why I'll write it, because I *want to* and I MUST!"

"I do consider how you feel!" he cried. "I do!" But his voice was shredded by anxiety, hope, and guilt, and her lips came together in the profile of a razor blade.

" I   do   not   want   to   fight   comma   there are things   to   be   said   comma and comma   we   will   forget   my   writing period."

He was becoming more and more shaken, and as Alice was

biting her lip in near tears of rage and frustration, a girl about
eight years old came into the kitchen, sniffling and yawning.

"Hi Daddy, Mommy can I have some orange juice?"

Alice nodded, tight lipped. She rose, created a glass of
orange juice which she handed to her daughter, and as Sally
sipped the juice she climbed into Nathan's lap. Alice cleared the
table as Nathan held a napkin to Sally's nose, and said "Blow."
She blew, he wiped her nose, which made her laugh, put the
napkin in an ashtray, and kissed the top of her head as she made
noises sipping the juice.

"How are you?" he asked, looking at Alice at the sink.

"Okay," she said. "Not so good. Are you coming again?
Soon?"

"As soon as I can," he answered.

"When is soon?"

"—Next week."

"Aw Daddy I know, but not sooner? Not Sunday?"

Alice turned from the sink, and yelled, "Tell her! Goddammit Nathan, TELL HER!"

"Sunday," Nathan said, terrified. "I—we—we'll have the
whole day together. You and me—and Matt."

Alice turned, fighting tears, and began washing dishes.

"Good," she choked.

Sally put the empty glass on the table, and Nathan rose
with her in his arms, and carried her into the bedroom, put her
in bed, and as she embraced and kissed him he tucked her in.
She said,

"Sunday."

"Sunday it is," he grinned, and after saying goodnight
and taking a look at Matt asleep in the next bed, Nathan went
into the living room and sat beside Alice on the sofa. She was
smoking a cigarette and looking through the TV Guide, face
like a tombstone. His face was covered with perspiration, but
he said—listen,

"Listen Alice, gee whiz I—I'm sorry."

She dropped the magazine, put her fists against her teeth, and with lowered head, said, in soft tones—

"I know you think of me, but what you don't understand about yourself is although you're aware of some of what I'm feeling, you're always too late to do or even say anything that will help, and when things happen you're not alert or even there, which forces me to be the one to take on-the-spot action. That's the spot you put me on, you drunken stinking son of a bitch, I'm raising these kids, not you—you go to your bars and fuck around while I'm up here trying to—no, no this isn't right and I'm wrong—again—I'm getting what I asked for, I asked for it, so I'm getting it, and I don't blame you, I don't, but somehow you're always too late, you react too late, and you leave me to handle things, and then you—you—you—" she whispered: "you irresponsible *bastard*—you're sorry, and guilty, oh how *easy* it is to be guilty! How easy! while doing nothing, and on top of all that pile of your own mess you're in, you expect me to still love your romantic illusion of yourself."

She took a deep breath for control, exhaled, breathed deep again, exhaled, wiped her eyes, looked at him, and said,

"Do you understand?"

He nodded, and put a trembling hand to his lips, stared down at the coffee table, and then at the television set. She rose to her feet, crossed the room, turned it on, found the channel, and as the screen brightened and came into focus she returned to the sofa and sat beside him, he who was not seeing much of anything next to her who was seeing almost everything, and both persons for those and other reasons, were frightened, hurt, and so angry they were speechless.

Commercials followed the logo, the program began and the storyline ran to the next commercial. Nathan began to fidget.

"Pretty low-level stuff," he growled, frowning.

"True," she murmured.

"Do you have any vodka?"

"I don't know," she said, "But I knew it. Why don't you look? You know where it is, you put it there. I haven't had any."

He rose, went into the kitchen, looked in the cupboard and found the quart, three quarters gone. He made a drink, a stiff drink, and returned to her, sat down and watched television fiction head to a commercial which was followed by more televised fiction followed by another commercial which preceded more fiction, as Nathan drank, yet almost choked in a sudden stepping barefoot on a scorpion realization, asked,

"Would you like something?" his heart in his mouth.

She looked at him, and for a moment didn't say anything. But as his hands began to shake, the ice cubes to clank and his cheeks to tremble, she said,

"Yes. Thanks. I think it's thanks. Is it thanks? Sure it is. Of course. Thanks. There, I said it," she spoke, in a voice that has been described as indicating rough seas ahead— "thank you, Nathan. How considerate. A little late, as usual, but, better, as the saying goes, better bait than be bit, there's some gin left. A light gin and tonic would be nice."

Taking his drink, or what was left of it, with him, he went into the kitchen, and as he made her drink, he made himself one too, having finished his first while making her first, this making of his second drink would, he realized, as a helpful gesture, kill two trips with one journey, his mind was as clear as the glasses that held the alcohol—all objects leaped into focus, everything had meaning, and the errand he was on was of geometrical perfection, so the drink he made for her was, he knew, perfect, and the one he made for himself was better than his first drink which had been perfect, the proof (aside from 80) being in the comparison, meaning, as he sipped his second he was aware of a wonder: above perfection, all the glow and precision of—a Purcell trumpet! and though he didn't fail to notice that there was enough for but one more drink left in the quart, which caused a jolt of anxiety, he yet calmed in the memory of what was left of Max's twenty, and was almost happy as he returned to her, because her neighborhood liquor store, which stayed open until midnight, was there at the other end of the telephone! *and* he had enough scratch to tip the delivery boy! *terrific:* he sat down, handed her the drink, and asked,

"Did I miss anything?"

She laughed.

"Yes. Me." Sipped her drink, murmured a note of pleasure, looked across at the tv set and said, "I don't know. I'm not watching."

"Well," he said. "I walked into that one."

"Um hum."

She curled her legs under her, and Matt walked into the room, to stand before his mother.

"Mommy, can I have some ice cream?"

"Is there any left?" she asked, distracted, but then clearing. "Look and see—help yourself, would you? Mom's tired."

Which he did, and while Nathan and Alice sipped their drinks and stared at one dimensional fiction and commerce, Matt got the ice cream he wanted, and returned with it, and spoon.

"Mommy?"

"No. Go to bed. Eat in your room."

Matt sat down next to his father, Alice sipped her drink, put it down, stood up, crossed the room quick-step, switched off the television, turned, and facing Matt and Nathan, said, voice rising—

"I'm up to here," her index finger across her throat, "with you. I am sick of pandering to *you,* and to *you.* I don't know why it is, but when *you* come up to visit, *you* take over this place—while I serve you! It's incredible! And—*you* breeze in here asking me for ice cream which in a normal circumstance I would get for you! Can anyone believe it? but having gotten what you want, indulgence indulged, you leave, so-long Mommy, so-long Alice, thanks a lot, while I do the dishes!"

Although the message was clear, it was in fact, too clear, as crystals crystallized it was over-clear, and because of that ultra-lucidity, it confused Nathan and Matt, both of whom sat open-mouthed, wide-eyed and astonished, each pointing a finger at his chest, saying, in one voice—

"Me? What did I do?"

"I'm going to bed," she said, and left the room.

A door slammed.

Matt looked at Nathan who looked at Matt, both trying to figure out what was quite clear. Matt, gesturing with his thumb—to her bedroom, whispered, to Nathan,

"What's with Mommy?"

Nathan whispered, "I don't know, but it's a good question—she's tired," he said out loud, thinking that were he a writer, to answer that common, and, to Nathan and Matt, reasonable little question, he would write a book, or perhaps two, but two wouldn't do it, nor, he realized, would three, or four—or five, but, his sense of humor not having left him, he would title it—WHAT'S WITH MOMMY? subtitled *An Encyclopedia Melancholia*.

"She's angry at us," Matt said, as Nathan put his arm around the boy, and agreed.

"Me first," Nathan said.

"Me second," Matt said.

"You said it," Nathan said.

"But I don't want it," said Matt.

"Me," said Nathan, "either," and they laughed. Nathan rubbed Matt's head suggesting he go to bed. Matt nodded, and putting saucer and spoon on the table, got to his feet.

"Sleep will cure your sinus," Nathan said, wondering where he got that little wisdom, then remembering his mother told him. Sleep cures almost anything, she had said, and Nathan felt a bit weird.

"Where'd you hear *that*?" Matt asked, laughing. "That's crazy!"

"I know," Nathan admitted. "My mother told me. Sleep cures almost anything. Quote, unquote."

"When was that?" Matt asked. "When you were at Valley Forge?"

"Yeah, and Mom was helping Martha with the flag. No, it was when I did that portrait of Washington."

They chuckled, said goodnight, but Matt turned in the doorway, and returned to Nathan.

"Dad?"

Nathan looked at his son, and Matt asked him if he could ask him a question. Sure.

"Who's Judy?"

"A girl I used to go with."

"Did—no, I shouldn't—"

"Mommy knew," Nathan said.

"Did she mind?"

"Yes and no."

"Why no?"

"I don't know, to be honest, but don't ask her."

"I think I know why I shouldn't ask, but—"

The conjecture hung, and Nathan said some questions don't want answers, and Matt asked what that meant, and Nathan said Well, some questions answer themselves, because in certain cases or situations, it's wise to let a question remain so it can find its own answer.

Matt nodded, and said he thought he understood, adding, "But if you find out, will you tell me?"

"Maybe," Nathan said.

"Aw Dad, that means you already know." Matt smiled, but he was hurt.

But Nathan underwent a sudden shock, realizing he was hearing Alice's deductive thinking in his son's language, and as a sharp jab, was jealous, yet he realized her influence was healthy, and not to be envied, but supported, which thought caused him discomfort and a pang of something he wasn't sure—was. But, he realized, in truth he was jealous, but what man wouldn't be jealous of Alice? She was—let's face it. She had more of everthing than any other woman he had known, read about, seen on the silver screen, or—Matt watched his father thinking, and his—Matt's—hurt turned into curiosity and a good question.

"What are you thinking?" he asked.

"I'm thinking that your mother has—influenced you in a good way."

"Yeah?" Matt grinned. "How?"

Wasn't that Alice speaking? Nathan thought, and laughed, "I'll tell you on Sunday."

They smiled to each other, Matt weighing this certain adult tactic, while Nathan watched Matt—"Sunday," Nathan said. "It's late, Matt."

"True," Matt smiled, they embraced, and Matt went to his room, but as Nathan finished his drink and got to his feet, in a seriousness he wasn't used to feeling, but which characterized him at work, it came very clear, as an objective thought, that he was divided, and that it was (this came in a deep rush), it was crucial that he be alone, that he clean his loft, and confront his work—the two big ones—as well as blank canvases. No bars, no girls, no more reading spy thrillers. No more escape until the canvases started talking.

He went into Alice's bedroom. She was sitting up in bed, reading. He sat on the edge of the bed beside her. Her face was worn, and sad.

"Alice," he said.

"What."

"I—" he gestured.

"Everything you say begins in the first person."

He took her hand, she put down the book, and they held hands.

"I'll tell Matt to get his own ice cream and juice—tomorrow," Nathan said.

"Why didn't you tell him while you were talking out there?"

"I didn't—think, of it."

She pursed her lips as he rose, went into Matt's room and told the boy, returned and sat beside Alice again.

"Thank you," she said. "Although, as usual, a little—but no matter."

"Was it something special that made you blow up?"

"At you and Matt? No, I don't think so. It came as, shall we say, a realization? You did the little things and I did and still do, the big things. You made me a good drink, you're good at that, and which effort is about as hard for you as stepping off a rug, but I have to clean up out there, bring the saucer, silverware, glasses, etc., back, wash and put them away, or, for example you won't be here tomorrow to follow through with what you just told Matt, and he'll be like he always is, just as you will. Matt's all right," she amended.

"I know he is," Nathan said. "You're being cruel to me."

"I suppose I am," she said.

"You're tired, aren't you."

"Yes, it was a long day."

"What happened?"

Her lips parted in astonishment, but then she saw what he meant. "I'm sorry, Nathan. I'm talked out . . ." her voice dwindled.

He shook his head. "I'm sorry I was late. I miss your

clock/radio.''

"I know," she said. "And there's a metaphor in there which I understand. But it doesn't help, nor does your regret. You'll do it again.''

"Are we going to begin to fight again? What round is this?''

"I don't know. Are we?''

"Do you want me to leave?''

Her eyes got dark, and hard, and in the sequence, shot sparks.

"Do you want to?" she asked.

"Do you want me to?" he asked, angry and alarmed because he knew he was making a serious, albeit classical mistake, yet he was divided—he wanted to stay, he wanted to go.

"It's up to you," she said.

He almost—almost—said he was divided, but checked himself, then realized she knew anyway, yet wise caution stilled his tongue. He said, "I don't want to go, but if you're going to be like this, I don't want to stay, and as you want me to be aware of you and how you're feeling, I want to know what you want, so tell me.''

"Maybe you'd better go," she said, with, were she face to face with a copperhead, a smile to paralyze it. In her test of Nathan. Yet she was very near tears, because she wanted him to stay.

But at that point, he was confused in a way he couldn't handle, but even in his sure uncertainty of what was happening, he refused to use his painting as an excuse, although it was true, and Alice again had been right, truth is tricky, but in the end his painting was his, it was personal, and his alone, so in trying to find a solution through himself he was insecure to a point of danger, and feeling panic, he yet knew a decision had to be made, and in that light a decision was formed, and when he

83

said it he was angry at their circumstance rather than her, because she knew he would leave, and too late he realized she knew. She wasn't reading his mind, she was following his habits, and as he was so predictable, it was easy for her, which Nathan felt was unfair, he therefore felt trapped, victimized and in that sequence, angry. It was a pity he couldn't say that sequence, for she would have agreed, as no doubt she didn't like what she was doing either, knowing Nathan was insecure, the expression on his face told her he felt trapped, so with her he was without her, and habit or not, she realized it was quite possible she was forcing him to leave, against both their wishes, but then, at bottom she knew they shared a near violent truth, thus in a true way, he had to go. It was vital he be alone, and that she too be alone, which truth caused a deeper and while courageous—more far reaching sadness than she'd known. She'd felt it before, but this realization seemed to penetrate clear through her—the keys to their future were in being alone, and as she was forming the words to speak, he rose, and with a hurt, and angry expression said,

"Then I Goddammed will go."

He crossed to the door, opened it, turned, and looked at her. The expressions on their faces formed a complicated and profound tableau of two people being torn apart, yet poised in space, beyond words which, were they attempted, had better be the right ones, because he as well as she, for their own different reasons, was losing control.

"I'll call, and I will spend Sunday with the kids."

"Fine," she said, in a hurt and lethal exhaustion. "I'll see you then."

"Okay," and he left.

But before he left, just before he altogether left, he—like the man in the cartoon, tip-toed into the kitchen, to the cupboard, and drinking straight from the bottle, finished it, and beginning the gesture to put the empty on the little kitchen table, his hand paused midair, he held up the index finger of the other hand, shook his head, and whispered "No no," crossed the kitchen, and put the empty in the trashcan, knowing it was a fine illustration of what Alice had meant all evening, but in another perception, as he hadn't eaten much that day, what Alice had meant all evening faded into a clear perception of reality: that second drink, the cosmic one of Purcell's trumpet had hit him, and standing in the elevator, holding the railing, he realized he was dizzy, and, in fact, a little drunk, a little drunk? He was drunk, and in the rationalized universe of said circumstance, as he got out of the elevator, and crossed the lobby, it was clear that the clearest way to get lucid again, was to have another drink, and remembering that pleasant little bar around the corner, where he and Alice had of recent met, and she had introduced him to the bartender (a nice, but sort of low-level guy), and Nathan had wondered what ex-husbands wonder, but, no matter, in he went, and down he sat at the bar, said hi to the bartender, ordered the drink, paid for it, put his elbows on the bar and his face in his hands, stared into the drink, and thought in whispers, murmurs, and mutters.

"What an asshole I am! But did she want me to stay? Yes, but maybe no! Probably both. Like me. But—who would want to be with her when she's like that? But—who would want to be with me when I'm like—decisions decisions, I'll call her tomorrow, I'll wait to call Hartmann, he can wait too, am I running out on her again? Yes, but I have to be alone. So, I am not. I'm doing what I have to do! Or am I? She—I—could have stayed, but God I don't want to, yet I wanted to. She needs me, and the kids do too—am I a man or a baby, running away from something unpleasant—yes, again. What should I have done?"

He sipped the drink, frowning and thinking, as his head cleared a little, about her saying he was irresponsible, which he knew was true. She's right, he thought. I am. But isn't that what I am? I'm not a magician, I don't pull irresponsibility out of a hat, I'm irresponsible, like a rabbit's a rabbit. I'm a rabbit, start hopping old hare, and get busy painting.

He finished his drink and ordered another.

As for Judy, he thought anew, there will be no more Judy—not for me. To hell with her. Let her go her way! Good for her! Bon Voyage, and best of luck, young fuck! I'll call her tomorrow and tell her I never want to see or speak to her again, and if she gets in my way I'll kick her teeth in.

He was therefore angry, and as he drank his drink his eyes developed a hard inward stare, the door opened and Alice walked in, very handsome in her pale rage, dark blue jacket, with collar up, belted at the waist.

"Alice!" cried Nathan, in disbelief, having had visions of letting Judy have it *bam* he had forgotten Alice, and—he almost said Hi! How are you? with a smile! but his metabolism changed—again, for it had operated in him à la Judy and seeing Alice changed in the shock of it, for he was glad to see Alice, not having though of her of recent, yet his blood ran cold when she turned, and her eyes met his. Her hands were in her jacket pockets, she walked over to him, and said,

"It doesn't bother me that you ran out again, or that I know it's important for you to be alone—and for me too—or even that you won't change, but what infuriates me is you *asked* me."

But Nathan, in another surprise, as he had been thinking of Judy in terms of his fist, it flashed into him that when she Judy had left him at that bar, she had asked if it was okay? and Nathan's body felt what can be described as Continental Drift, for he felt colossal and frantic. Adrift.

"But Alice!" he said— "Did you want me to stay or didn't you? I didn't—still don't know!"

She curled her lips in such a way he saw her teeth.

"That," she said, "is not the point."

"But what IS the point? I'm confused!"

"Do you think," she said, pointing at him, her eyes direct on his, "do you think I'm going to tell you? You *and* X-number of OTHER MEN?" she cried. "Do you think I'm going to explain it to you like your *mother?* Well I'm not, and I'm not your mother, that bar where you go is, and your sister Judy too."

"I don't go there anymore!"

"Then suffer," Alice cracked, "while you figure it out for yourself, if you can, but meanwhile," she snarled—"*get out of here, this is my bar.*"

Nathan's lips trembled and his hands shook. He looked at her as if he'd never seen her before, in horror, and shock, his emotions like a cyclone as he heard himself say, in a voice he wasn't familiar with—

"Okay, okay, I'll go after I finish this."

"Good," she said, turned, and walked to the other end of the bar, sat down, greeted the bartender and ordered a drink. Nathan, aware he was the center of attention for all the bar, blushed as he finished his drink, left a tip, rose from his bar stool, walked outside and took the subway home, but the ride was an angry and baffling one, for he felt betrayed, somehow used, hurt, anxious, guilty, and shaken in body, mind and soul. He paced the floor of the moving machine. He sat down, stood up, mumbled, muttered, whispered and talked out loud to himself as he rubbed his face, head and neck in intense agitation, the train pulled into the station, he got off, crossed the platform all in a dream, went through the turnstile, turned left and ran up the steps so preoccuped he didn't notice Judy coming down them, towards him, herself preoccupied, and in thought walking slow, so when they collided, and saw each other, the look on Nathan's face wiped out her smile of greeting, and turned her face into a mask of fear, as Nathan screamed—

"YOU! YOU! *VALENTINE'S EVE!*"

Grabbing for her, but missing as she jumped backwards up a step, he followed her as she retreated, until they were on the sidewalk, and passers-by looked at them as Judy backed away from him, her eyes wide, face white and hands out, pleading with him, as his right fist clenched jerked before his chest and he gestured with his left, disregarding everyone including two cops in a parked squadcar, not twenty feet away.

"Why did you lie to me? *That's* what hurt so!"

"I DIDN'T!"

"Yes you did," he said, enraged, "that—no more sex because you might hurt me bullshit, that *was* a lie!"

"IT WASN'T!"

He caught her right hand and drew her close, but she was nimble, and broke free, and as he advanced she backed away, crying out her plea—

"I didn't want to hurt you! I still don't!"

"That compounds the lie, Goddammit, because the truth was you wanted to get rid of me and didn't know how, so no more sex would work. I know I was getting too close to you, and that you wanted out—but you didn't need to lie. Admit you did! ADMIT IT!" he yelled.

They stopped, and faced each other. She lowered her head and said, as she wept,

"Yes, it's true. You wanted too much of me, your influence was too strong, and I—I couldn't, I—wanted out. You were so crazy!"

"And that adventure crap was your cover. All right, baby, you've *got* it, but understand that I know you would have left me no matter what words you used, you would have left any man, as long as you get your way you don't care what you say, and you wanted to stay friends—stay FRIENDS! FRIENDS! so when you made your final move—ADMIT IT—the breakaway would be smooth for you, you ambitious and arrogant bitch, trying to smooth something so painful, my God I didn't mean anything to you, so from here on in you mean *nothing* to me, in fact you mean less—"

She tossed her head in panic, and with her arms out from her sides, said—

"I know you're angry, and you're right, it's true. I have to forget you. I have to live my life—I'm sorry Nathan. I did lie and I didn't—don't—know, what to say," she wept.

He stepped to her, raised her chin in his left hand, and held his fist in her face.

"That's more like it, but I don't trust those tears. I know you, you told me, remember?"

She nodded her head.

"So listen sister, steer clear of me. You left me for adventure—in my bar, well you can have it, but there will be no more adventure with me, and there will be no more talking. I never want to see you or speak to you again, nor you to me. You're dead to me. Get it?" and like the flashback in the bar Nathan envisions himself and Judy in the bar, laughing with the bartender, as he, Nathan, says—"Get it?" and she, delighted, points a finger in Nathan's happy face, cries—"I got it!"

"I got it," Judy whispered, "But I—I don't want—"

"That's right. You don't want, you bet you don't want, but you did want, and so you lost me, well go use somebody else, because I don't want you anywhere *near* me, and if you try to make contact in any way, you get this—"

Holding his fist in her face.

"—I'll send you home for a visit so fast you won't know where you came from."

"But Nathan, I—"

"No nothing, no buts, and no Nathan, ever again."

"BUT NATHAN!"

"Get away from me."

"I want you to be happy—I do, I want you to," she

sobbed.

"Sure you do, to lessen your guilt and make things smooth again so you can go your way and—maybe, just maybe use me again, some day, well GO your way, go find out what love is, and you'll understand what I'm feeling."

"But I don't think," she choked—"I ever will!"

"Then you'll suffer, you two-faced manipulator, and I hope you burn in hell for it."

He walked down the street, striking his right fist into his left palm, mumbling curses while she went to the wall of a building, a bank, in fact, and leaned against it, put her face in her hands, and wept, while passers-by glanced, and the two cops in the squad car watched, in silence, their faces set. Then each shook his head.

Instead of going home, Nathan was so mixed up and angry he continued walking until he came to a small bar, went in, and ordered a drink. Stolichnaya, in fact. He and the bartender were friends, and the bartender, a big clean-shaven guy who owned the bar, owned a stammer, too, and after Nathan had said Stolichnaya, the bartender said,

"The aay-eighty?"

"The eighty," Nathan said, rubbing his face as Bill, the bartender, made the drink, and after giving it to Nathan, wiped the bar in front of him, leaned on it and asked, stammering on the soft H, as well as vowels, how things were going.

"I can't paint."

"Don't you have a show coming up?"

"September."

Bill thought a little, and said, "Thaaaat's four an aaa half months—?"

"Yeah, seems fine, doesn't it, but—well, I might go west with Max and do a batch of small pictures . . . but there are the kids. I don't know what I'm going to do. And I've got to get some money. A lot of money."

90

"Are the kids oh-okay? Hhhow's Alice?"

Nathan laughed. "Are they okay? Where shall I begin? The kids are sick and if Alice had her way I'd be in little pieces from here to the Metropolitan."

"My ex-wife," Bill began, "had a temper. She fooled you. She was built like a hummingbird but at heart was a grizzly, and the oh-only way I could handle her was to slug her or leave her, and ay-ay-I most often slugged her before I left her, until she left mmm-me," he grinned, and they laughed.

"Sounds good," Nathan smiled. "I just saw Judy," and Nathan held up his right fist and looked at it, "I wanted to paste her so bad my fist hurts from frustration."

"Wh-why didn't you?" Bill asked. "She's still young."

"I don't know, of course I know. I couldn't, I could have, but maybe, I mean I—well, wanted to threaten her, I'm too fucked up to start slugging girls, and it wouldn't have been the point, anyway, and on top of that, I'd have been wrong."

"You mean you weren't ready."

"I almost was," Nathan smiled, "and if tonight won't do it, I don't know what will. But you're close—I wasn't ready. Thanks."

"Yuu-you're welcome," Bill said, "do you want to pay for this or shall I take dictation?"

"You know shorthand?"

Bill walked to the cash register, saying over his shoulder, "For you Nay—Nathan, I know shorthand."

Let's say that they talk, there are other people at the bar and a pool game is going on in the background when the door opens and a young guy comes in, and seeing Nathan, stops, throws out his arms, cries NATHAN! who turns, the young guy walks over and they embrace, and talk with much warmth and enthusiasm—the young fellow had been a student of Nathan's, at the same school where Nathan had met Judy. His name is Gregory, and after Nathan introduces Greg to Bill, they drink and talk. Greg is in town for a few days and has tried to find Nathan, without success, so is delighted to see him here, thus they continue until the bar closes, Bill locks up and the three men sit in back and talk and drink until the wee hours when they at last head home. Greg is unhappy about the state Nathan is in, so when they say farewell on the street it is a moving scene. Greg walks across town to the apartment where he and his girl friend are staying, and Nathan heads north to his loft, staggering inside and up the steps, not seeing, in the darkness, the small pile of folded messages on the floor under the mail slot. Notes from friends with the name of the man from Pittsburgh, and the telephone number. So the next day is Thursday and Nathan wakes with a start, puts on his glasses, and cries,

"Today is Thursday!"

He rubbed his face with both hands—he looked terrible—and as he stared across the loft he made a fist, and shook it in the air, saying—

"I'm going to sell this Goddammed place to Dom and go to Taos with Max. I'll do a couple of small paintings and a batch of watercolors, and with these—" gesturing across the loft to the huge two paintings on the opposite wall—"That'll be *it! FUCK IT!"*

He got out of bed, and sorting through dirty clothes strewn across the loft, found some things that didn't smell so bad, and so he dressed, but not without difficulty, for he had forgotten he had a hangover, which he soon would realize, but for the moment he was all business—

Okay, here it gets complicated so I'll give you a sloppy synopsis, and the storyteller sipped his drink as we watched, waiting, while he considered his delivery.

What I want is an original sense of detail, like the scenes of Judy painting, an indigenous sense of the painter in his world, as Nathan makes coffee and sits at the table in the kitchen area which is a mess, but a detailed mess, and then takes pencil and paper and makes a list of things to do, and of the people he owes money to, talking out loud as he writes, arriving at the conclusion he wants, he has to get out of town. He then leaves his building, ignoring the new mail which has covered the notes from friends the day before, goes to the phone booth on the corner and phones Dom, they arrange the sale, Nathan getting a thousand in cash up front the next day—Friday afternoon—and the rest in a check on Monday, so Nathan, having made a decision at last, is relieved, so he calls the landlord, and the gas and electric company, both of which agree to his three-quarter payment within forty-eight hours, and the remainder next week. He phones Max and tells him the news, that they can leave when Dom's check clears, which, being deposited on Monday afternoon, will clear on Thursday. And Nathan can draw cash on Friday, so they will leave next Friday afternoon. That sounds good to Max, and during the week Nathan can get all his affairs straight, which Max advises, meaning, in particular, Alice and the kids, so it is a different Nathan that steps from the telephone booth. His eyes have a light, and his face is determined. He has made a decision, come what may, on which he will stand. One has to take risks, big risks, in life, and this is a big one, so he rushes home, and on the way hears his name being called, he stops, turns, and it is Greg, running toward him, in great haste.

"Nathan! Listen! A guy from the Carnegie's in town looking for you—"

"That's all I need," Nathan said.

Greg's face fell, but he gathered himself—

"You are," he admonished Nathan, "in no shape to start that wisecracking shit. Gary says this guy used the word *imperative*, that it is *imperative* that you call him and that he sees you, as he goes back to Pittsburgh tomorrow night—don't you know the whole town's been looking for you? Didn't you get the notes?"

"What notes—the Carnegie doesn't want me. They've got me, and how come you guys from out of town always have the latest word! I've been in this Goddammed place for over twenty years, and it *never* fails!"

They entered Nathan's building.

"Look! There they are—under your mail, the notes!" Greg pointed, and bending picked one up, gave it to Nathan who unfolded it and put it in his pocket saying collectors were no news to him and he had nothing to show the guy anyway.

"So," Nathan said to Greg— "You went to the bar."

"Well," Greg said, lowering his eyes, but then looking at Nathan— "Judy wanted to see Dorothy."

"And?"

"Oh come on, you know they're good friends. You know what's going on, hey Nathan, come on, phone this guy," Greg smiled, "and see what he says."

They walked back to the telephone booth on the corner as Greg explained that he had gone to the bar with Dorothy, but when Judy and Dorothy were together at a table Greg sat at the bar and talked with Gary, the bartender, and Nathan's name came up, thus too the man from Pittsburgh, and Greg had left right away to come up here and find Nathan—and after discovering Nathan hasn't eaten yet, Nathan, with some money he borrowed from Bill the night before, gives Greg ten and Greg is to shop for eggs, liver, bread, juice etc., and Nathan says he'll phone, adding no matter what happens he's selling the loft to Dom and next week will go west with Max.

But Greg is stunned—speechless, until he finds the words he wants—

"You're going to sell that loft? but Nathan, that's—that's *madness*. You love that loft, that loft is your *life*, what you— loved in Alice and your children. Don't *do* it, please—wait—

see what Pittsburgh says, okay? Please—promise me."

"All right," Nathan agrees, "you're right, it can't hurt, I can change my mind, Dom will understand, and it's good thinking to boot."

"To boot," Greg laughed, adding—"I'll boot you if you don't—"

Nathan phones the man while Greg shops, but the man isn't at his hotel, so Nathan leaves the number of the bar, hangs up, calls the bar and tells the bartender—Gary—to expect a call, Gary taking the number of the telephone booth just in case. Nathan says he'll phone every hour—details details details—and Nathan waits for Greg outside the telephone booth on the sidewalk while various people use the public phone, and as Greg, with groceries, comes into view a couple of blocks away, the phone rings, Nathan answers it and Gary says Mr. Pittsburgh just called, and was there a message Nathan could give him? Nathan says tell the guy to be at his loft at eleven tomorrow morning, Gary says lemme know what happens. Nathan says, you'll be the first to know, and after Gary says he Nathan sure is sentimental, they hang up, Greg joins Nathan, and on the way to the loft, Nathan fills Greg in—Greg is certain something great will happen, but Nathan is doubtful, yet thoughtful, and admits it's possible. So they go to Nathan's loft, have something to eat and Greg helps him clean the place up, and, later that night, around ten, while Nathan and Greg and Dorothy watch tv, nip vodka and relax, there's a scene at the bar that bothers me, the storyteller frowned.

What is it? Blaze asked.

It isn't important, but it's necessary.

Painters in their bar, of a critic critical of Nathan's work, and of that critic's disciples, of young women painters and of young women and how guys treat them, of the great and the petty jealousies, competition, backbiting, friendship, fun, and danger—the heavy alcoholics, and the un-healthy mixed in with neighborhood people, and the virtuous intellectuals who make a bottle of beer last three hours—not that any of this matters, but—there's something in the night after night after night necessity—the utter actuality just by being in their continuity, their routine, right there. It includes violence revealing their dark side, their resentments and occasional potential insanity which can lead to danger, as well as their other side—the light, amusing, bright and witty rascals—in short, a world of its own which has never been given the narrative the great story that it is deserves, but—being ignored—exists in clichés and stereotypes I loathe because they're all lies. Lies that live, and thrive, because they are lies that work for the businesses that manipulate them. For example, with rare exceptions, painters are still considered neurotics, anarchists, beret, cape and cane-carrying Bohemians—more crazies in our crazy society—which the media use to no end. But at center, in the art world, as in any profession, there are loyalties. No matter what happened between Nathan and Dom, Dom would understand, because Dom was concerned about Nathan. That's the good side, but, as in any profession—for example the law—there's the other side. As well as there are men and women painters who have nine-to-five jobs, or who teach, or, as many learn a profession—are electricians, plumbers, interior or exterior house painters, carpenters, or who are parent-supported, it's a struggle for survival most aren't aware of—these, have their opposite, too, the painters who aren't, in a strict sense, crooks, but in a generalization say a little illicit. The imitators, the copycats, one has no idea of the scale of imitation that goes on, by the copycats who in a little tilt, might well be called crooks. And then too, the pretenders and off persons who want to get inside the art world which affords them an identity they otherwise wouldn't have—the crooks we hear and read about in the papers, the big crooks, domestic and international in their reach, we know about them, and to a painter in his or her everyday sense—part of the CBS Evening News, but on the inside of that painter's day-by-day life, he or she is day by day aware of a certain sinister characteristic of their life, involving in a general sense, crime, drugs for example, as well as—in a literal sense—theft, and as this is involved in their lives, there's a paradox along with it, as certain gangsters and detectives who enjoy the company of artists, as well as the punks, the hustlers and the creeps—it's a good chance, and it is, that the painter knows the thief who stole his paintings, it's a better chance that they met in the bar, and if somebody, which I'd wanted to do, would give that bar its due, the world would know a truth heretofore hidden in a colossal, and damned near premeditated lie. I wanted to have a scene of that truth.

If I don't hear more about that man from Pittsburgh, Blaze said, I am going to do one of my 100 proof Stolichnaya freakouts. Please, friend, what happens next?

It's Friday, the next day, and that gentleman showed up at Nathan's loft at eleven, they shook hands, and Mr. Barkis, the man from Pittsburgh, Mr. Henry Barkis, was delighted to meet Nathan, who was—Nathan was—clean shaven and appeared to be together. Mr. Barkis, who was in no way of being anything but together, glanced around the loft, and asked Nathan if those two big paintings were—it?

"They're it," Nathan said. "So far this year."

Mr. Barkis then wandered up and down before each painting, giving each careful scrutiny, nodding his head, and after having gotten the exact measurements from Nathan, and jotting in his notebook he smiled, and turning to Nathan, who was cleaning up his paint table in such a way, as is proper, in these matters, that he seemed disinterested.

"Yes," Mr. Barkis said, "these will do. They're great. I like what you're onto. Very fresh. Original. New in the best sense."

He crossed the loft to Nathan's paint table, and as Nathan

smiled as one smiles to one's landlord, the other man said,

"Barkis is willing," and gave Nathan a pointed look, but seeing no response, shrugged. Nathan said—

"Well, I'm glad you're willing, and am happy you like my paintings, but I'm thinking about my gallery and my show in September—everything I paint will be based on these two."

Mr. Barkis smiled like surgeons smile before easy operations,—a sort of smirk—and said, "Excellent, but I'm not thinking about your gallery or the good man who owns it, whom I've known for years, and done business with. Nor am I thinking about you, or—September. I'm thinking about me, and I want those paintings."

Nathan said, to himself, but out loud, "What a paradox."

"Paradox?"

"Personal."

"I see. Let me explain, Mr. Fierce. I'm having a sort of retreat built, on the property in back of the main house, so I can get away from my home-routine and still be at home. It won't be finished until the end of October, the architect is drawing up the plans, and he asked what size I wanted the south wall to be, and I told him I had to see what new work you had first, which is why it was and is imperative that I contact you, because my little retreat is waiting, and I won't have to commission you, which I didn't want to do, it will therefore be built around these two paintings which will be in your show in September, around which you will build the rest of your show and I my retreat, so in that sense we share an experience—mine for life, yours for eternity."

"I can't sell out of my loft," Nathan said. "You know how it works. You know Arthur. I have a contract."

"Let me remind you again that I am not thinking of any of that. I know indeed how it works. I also know Arthur, but you don't seem to understand that I want those paintings. You are, to me, the best painter around—I love linear work, and your

98

draftmanship is the best, in my opinion, and my opinion is aggressive in this case, because I don't care how it or anything else works, including contracts. I care for nothing but how I work, and as I work for me, I work hard. I want those paintings."

Barkis laughed. A low laugh. Nathan made a note not to tell him of the trip west. Nathan said,

"I see," which meant he wanted to hear what Barkis would say next.

"I'll give you," Barkis said, "twelve thousand five hundred for both."

"No," Nathan said. "Seventeen five."

"All right, thirteen, no more and I mean it. I brought some cash with me—painters have a funny love of cash sales—and I'll give you a check for the rest, which, being as it's early on this Friday, you can still deposit. And don't lecture me about Arthur. If I bought them from him—say if I bought them from him at what—twenty thousand? Twenty-five? Come come, Mr. Fierce, it's basic mathematics, Arthur taking sixty percent . . . you might be a little honest about this. You might," he cleared his throat, "consider yourself fortunate." Barkis paused, and then added—"And you know how to handle it."

"Sure," Nathan said, voice casual, as well as his face, but in thought he was alarmed and shaken: was he going to tell Arthur the truth? If Arthur charged those prices Barkis just quoted, which he probably will, the difference will be considerable, and, as perspiration appeared on Nathan's brow, it would have to come, if it came at all, from—

"See here, Mr. Fierce," Mr. Barkis said, in a soft voice, "be reasonable. Your sales are down. You know. The market has changed, which you also know. Think a moment." Barkis glanced at the ceiling: "Keep these lights burning, Mr. Fierce," and after a pause—"my trucker will call you regarding the shipment—on me."

"I need cash," Nathan said.

"How about fifteen little ones, and a check for the rest."

"Swell? Great? Wonderful? How wonderful it's gonna be when I have to tell Arthur—also, I didn't know guys like you used language like that."

"If people who handle money don't know the language of money, they don't, in an aesthetic sense, deserve to have the money that creates the language, besides, slang is easier to speak, not so many syllables, and as thirteen grand isn't much to me—but is to you—we'll say I can afford to speak as I please."

He smiled, as a man smiles on the first taste of peppermint, and counted fifteen one-hundred dollar bills onto Nathan's paint table, and with his pen—a German fountain pen—wrote a check for the rest, which he handed Nathan, and said—

"I have an appointment in an hour-and-a-half, so, is there a good restaurant near? Where I may take you to lunch?" He was almost beaming. "Having gotten what I came for, as planned, I'll be delighted to," he grinned, "take you to lunch, although first, I imagine, you'd like to stop by your bank. Right?" Barkis asked, merrily.

Thus they leave, Nathan going to his bank, deposits the check, and then to lunch where they have cocktails, talk and eat, Nathan discovering, to his intense amusement, that Barkis' business card was a phony, used but for mere effect, as Barkis had worked there several years before, but kept his business cards when he quit. While they ate, Barkis spoke—

"I should confess that I'm not a *real* collector, but one who buys things he considers the best, and I buy them here and there, for example three years ago I gave my wife a signed first edition of *Tristram Shandy*—one of her favorite books. I got to know Arthur because of your work, and when you visit me when I unveil my retreat, I'll show you something you might have forgotten. It's in the main house, and its setting is perfect. When you visit, I'll show you, and you can also see where and how I live. You must meet my wife, she loves your work too—she read, if you'll forgive me, your ex-wife's novel, as did I, it's an excellent work. Sensitive, yet strong. I'm sorry about the divorce. It must have been painful for you both."

"It still is," Nathan said.

"If it isn't, it wasn't worth it in the first place." Barkis paused, and as if speaking something to himself, something which he knew by heart, said, "I have a few beautiful things. A little Rembrandt drawing, and a most unusual Gauguin, among others. Do you remember a small red painting you did, about ten years ago? Fourteen inches square?"

"So *you're* the guy who got that! Jesus, where have I been? I should have known, *you* were the guy from western Pennsylvania nuts about my work! But—why didn't you buy the big ones, why that little one? That was a great show!"

"True, but the little one was the best one."

"No it wasn't," Nathan said, "in—in the room to the right as you come in the gallery, I had—"

"A blue and white painting where you used cobalt and Prussian blues like few before you, and none since."

"*That* was the painting!" Nathan exclaimed.

"To you it was," Barkis smiled, "and it almost was, but you over-painted in the lower left corner, and flattened your transparency, remember, but in the little red one transparencies flow in perfection, as in the best of Pollock, and there is, as we know, no better than the best of Pollock."

Both men smiled. Barkis said—

"The little red one is as good as the best of Pollock."

"You're right—thanks—you're right about that over-painting. I forgot, Jesus it drove me crazy—as a matter of fact I learned something there. Maybe I will visit you. I've missed that little picture, and I'm gettin' curious."

Barkis smiled. "Still learning. Well, let me satisfy your curiosity and welcome you to my home."

Then Barkis frowned, and looked at Nathan as from afar, as

if seeing through him to a distant point, and it was to that point he spoke—

"Great painters know they're great because their work tells them so, and the lesser painters, who are every bit as important as their Masters, because the lesser ones form the milieu of continuity and influence, paint toward conviction, which is why their work shows conviction. But greatness includes conviction, and takes terrible risks. There are exceptions, of course," he chuckled. "There are always exceptions. But, in any event, I like the best and I like saying so. Nothing, I say, but the best for me! Therefore, I am very pleased to meet you at last. Until a few weeks ago, I had a lengthy and complicated problem—which I've cleared up, thank God, so I came here in eager anticipation, which opportunity my retreat has given me. Rather unique, don't you believe? Almost perfect, in fact."

He paused, sipped wine, and spoke again.

"It is perfect. You'll see my little collection. Some by unknowns, too, but they are the best." He looked into Nathan's eyes, "And so are you. Because you," raising the glass to Nathan— "*you* are the painter."

They shook hands on the sidewalk, and as a cab pulled up to the curb in response to Mr. Barkis' signal, Barkis said,

"Remember what Chekov said."

"Chekov said a lot of things."

"True, but among them you might recall—'Money, like vodka, can do strange things to a man.'"

They laughed as Nathan opened the back door for him, and Barkis getting in said,

"You know how Stalin drank his vodka."

"Ice cold, straight, with black pepper."

Barkis closed the door, and rolled down the window.

"It was fine meeting you. I'll look forward to seeing you again in the fall—good luck with your work."

"Thanks."

They waved—once—in farewell, and went their separate ways: the one man by taxi and the other on foot. Each had a different smile. The walking one of thought coupled with irony, and the one on wheels gazing through the windshield as if seeing a distant mountain top, and happy at the sight, smiled as if he owned it, not a little smug.

So here, the storyteller said, turning pages, are more details. Nathan goes home and begins cleaning his loft, paint table and brushes, which takes him most of the afternoon, and after having shopped, done the laundry, and in person paid the gas & electric company, as prearranged, then made several important telephone calls, and that evening has a good supper, after which he tackles his bills and makes a list of things to do the next day—Saturday—wash and wax the floor, wash the windows, write letters, also making a note for Sunday morning, before he will go up to see Matt and Sally, to begin to prepare for the trip west—what clothes and materials to take, etc., so around midnight Nathan goes to Bill's bar, pays his tab, and as arranged, sits at the bar with Greg and his girl friend Dorothy who had waited for him, and Nathan tells them what had happened, which news delights them, but when Nathan says how much money he paid out, and how much he still owes, they're a little deflated, and further so at what paint, canvas and stretchers will cost, as he'll be broke again, and won't be able to tell his gallery dealer, therefore he's going to sell the loft and go west, which angers Greg, and Dorothy too. They plead with him not to, Greg—: sublet the loft, and take things as they come, spend the spring and summer painting in Taos and wait and see what happens with the show! Does Arthur *have* to know? But Nathan is undecided, and Greg, who has become a little wild in his passion says it's wrong to sell that loft, it's wrong, *wrong,* too impulsive, it's—desperate!
And Greg, in sudden inspiration, takes Nathan by the

arm, and shakes him, saying, voice harsh—I was right before, wasn't I? Didn't I tell you to phone him? Didn't I tell you something would happen? *Trust me! Listen to me! I know! Nathan! I know!*—advice ringing true, causes Nathan to think. He nods. You're right, he says, but Goddammit I've *got* to get some money and Bill says C'mon, have a drink on me, you fucked-up artist, in fact I think I'll join y-y-you, being fucked-up myself.

The next day, Saturday, Nathan's up early, and begins doing the things he planned, but after he'd written letters and cards, washed the windows and mopped the floor, he threw down the mop saying enough, is enough, and went to the bar at the restaurant where he'd been with Mr. Barkis, wondering why Barkis had given him that look after saying he was willing to buy, and where had that quote from Chekov come from? Vell, he said, anyvay, imitating DeKooning, dot is a *good* quote, and sitting on a barstool in the middle of the bar, which was dark and almost empty, two or three couples finishing their lunches in the distance and no one but himself at the bar, Nathan falls into thought and realizes he's anxious—I'm anxious. I did everything except call Hartmann which I'll do—next week after I call mother, but how can I see Hartmann if I'm going west with Max? decisions, decisions, God, well, what to do? Fuck 'em, all—each and every one, why can't I have happy thoughts? After all, I've just sold the only two paintings I have and I'm broke—I'll make a will. In case something happens on the trip, so he gets paper and pen from the bartender, and sitting alone at the dark and deserted bar Nathan makes his will, mumbling leave everything to Alice and the kids, which he does, making a note to give it to his lawyer before he goes so the will can be drawn up and witnessed, etc., he returns the pen to the bartender and folds the paper, puts it in his jacket pocket, and with a sigh turns his gloomy face to the front of the place, and stares out the front window as human and mechanical traffic pass by, realizing, in a slow, slight sense of spooky spookily that he wasn't alone, that someone else was sitting at the bar, too, and around the far corner a woman sat near the wall, in semi-darkness, in a dark dress and jacket looking thoughtful, cool, neat, and nice. Very nice, in fact.

"Like a drink?" he asked.

"Sure," she said, and after the bartender had given it—a whiskey sour—to her, and Nathan had paid him, and the bartender had gone about the business bartenders go about, not appearing to notice Nathan, or the woman, which in that case was impossible because they were the only customers he had, yet as bartenders notice everything, if they're any good—if he had customers five deep at a packed bar he'd keep track of the guy who bought the drink as well as the woman who accepted it, because bartenders love a little snoopery, but when Nathan asked her,

"How are you doing?"
and she answered, "Not so well," the bartender still appeared not to notice. Her voice was husky.

"That's two of us," Nathan said.

"What were you writing?"

"My will," he said.

She laughed. "Your will? Are you going to die?"

"I might," he smiled. "I'm leaving town next week for Christ's sake and don't know where I'm going, I mean, I know where I'm going, but—"

"You don't know why."

"I don't," he mumbled. "I don't know why."

"Why are you?"

"I have to get out of town."

"That's too bad. Or is it?"

"May I join you?"

She hesitated. "Okay."

Nathan picked up his drink and the ice water chaser, and

joined her, while the bartender, head lowered as he put olives from a big jar into a rock glass, was watching with up-from-under eyes, as Nathan sat beside her, and heard them introduce each other, she saying she was flattered to meet Nathan complimenting him on his work, while not quite blushing or putting her finger at her throat, or playing with her pearls, she smiled, but of a sudden, didn't.

"What's wrong?" he asked. "I like you, but I just saw a dark cloud—"

"That dark cloud is my association to men, because of my bank veep ex-husband. He hated my creative friends."

"Well, my ex-wife hates my," Nathan paused, "creative friends, too, so we have two negatives in common."

"I didn't read her novel, but I heard it's excellent. I like you too. I like fast."

"Me too. It is, it's a terrific book. She's just finished another. I don't want to talk about her."

"I didn't mean—well, I—no more of *him*, either!"

"Say," he said, "not to sound an old movie, but what are you doing tomorrow night?"

"I'm leaving town in a couple of hours. My mother isn't well, and I won't be back until next weekend. But I'd like to see you again."

"Jesus," cursed Nathan, and felt himself on the brink, not so much of the decision, but its suddenness, thus his craziness was made more evident to him by the speed of his decision, which changed everything, so he asked her where she lived, and what her number was, which, he not having a paper, she wrote on the back of his will, which, excepting the part with her writing on it, he tore up while she laughed, and he grinned, putting the paper in his jacket pocket, and they relaxed, and talked the language, in that universal form, of that universal content, and she wiped her eyes with a hanky, blew her nose, gained control, and finished her drink.

"Bartender?" Nathan said. "Could we have two more?"

"Not for me—I have to go. I'm sorry, but I have to. Will you call me Friday evening?"

"We can spend next Saturday together."

"Yes," she smiled, her face happy. "That'll be fine," as she rose, took her coat off the back of her chair, and gave it to him, and he helped her put it on. She picked up her cigarettes and lighter which she put in her handbag, and held out her hand, which he took, and this was how it came to pass that they said goodbye, until Saturday, yet just before she left they stood for a moment, and while they were feeling what they were, they looked happy, from the bartender's point of view at the other end of the bar, as his two customers stood facing each other in shadows, as Nathan touched her cheek in gentle brevity, the bartender thought he saw—which in a blink was gone, a sort of glow around each of their heads, the bartender blinked again, and that was how two different men watched one woman walk away differently.

Nathan sits down, finishes his drink, orders another, and makes a mental list of things to do—call mother and get it over with, call Hartmann and make an appointment, call Alice, Dom, Greg, and, while he gets a couple of dollars worth of dimes and nickels, and walks towards the phone in front, he already hears Max's laughter, as Nathan drops the dime in, and dials, to tell Max the trip is off.

"Hey-lo," says Max.

"Max, Nathan, listen, I'm not going. I—well, I—quote you're not going to believe this, but, unquote—"

"I knew it," Max chuckles. "A chick."

"She's no chick, let me tell you. Can we get together? I can't talk on this abstraction."

"Okay. I'll drop by your place later, and, this being the sit-u-a-tion, I think I'll cut out tomorrow."

"Come on—wait a couple of days!"

"Nope, I'm packed and ready. See you later. . . ."

Nathan calls Dom and says he's staying in town and will keep the loft, Dom saying he's sure gonna miss that place, etc., Dr. Hartmann says Tuesday morning at ten will be fine, and Alice's recorded voice says she'll be back at six, please leave a message. When you hear the beep you have 60 seconds. Thanks. Here's the beep. Beeeep! Alice, I'm not going west, am keeping the loft, I see Hartmann on Tuesday, can't call mom, not yet but will, I'll tell you what's happening, very sorry about the other night, take care of yourself, I'll see you and the kids tomorrow, and as he hung up he heard her voice as he walked back to his seat at the bar, his body warm and humming, as Alice in his mind was saying several things, at the end of which was she was sorry about the other night, too, and she meant it.

But.

It goes fast from here. It's the new woman, and Nathan's painting. His loft is clean, neat and cool, yet warm— surrounded by his new work, flowers, plants, while she reads a novel on the bed, and he paints. He's finished four pictures, and he looks good. He looks happy.

On the far end of his painting wall, across the loft from the sleeping area and tv set, hang several framed nude drawings of her, above a stereo set, on the turntable of which is a record, and Sonny Rollins is his great strong self, yet in this instance sad, too, *You Don't Know What Love Is*, which has become their song. Sentimental? Deeply. The front door of the bar opened, and Audrey came in sneezing, followed by Dottie, both women very angry, and as they went towards Blaze, Lucky and the storyteller, as well as the shopping carts of groceries and laundry, they saw their husbands very intent in listening although well on their way to where everybody knew

Blaze and Lucky went while hearing a good story, rapidly, or slowly, it is in western Pennsylvania where Nathan and his sweetheart stand, drinking Mumm's, and talking with Mr. Barkis' wife, in Mr. Barkis' new retreat, which, having been finished later than was planned, caused the Barkises to have the unveiling coincide with Thanksgiving, therefore it is Thanksgiving Eve, and several dozen well-dressed persons stand around, nibbling lobster and drinking champagne, and talking, and from a distance far back from across the lawn, one saw a contemporary structure with one large glass wall, through which, on the opposite wall and on each side of the chimney and cheerful log fire, above the heads of the guests, Nathan's big paintings dominate Mr. Barkis' not so little retreat, in the precise way Mr. Barkis wanted, which he had told, and showed everyone, including Nathan.

Dottie was about to explode, while Alice watched a handsome man carving a turkey, and she smiled. Sensing it, he looked at her, and he too smiled. Pierre Boulez was conducting Handel's *Water Music* in the background, and Matt and Sally, sitting at the table, watched the bird being carved, mouths watering, and as they chattered their eyes were bright, they were great kids, really, I had no idea, nor did Blaze, that Audrey and Dottie were there, the fireworks surprised us out of our skulls, they came at us so swiftly, Judy was sitting at a large table, her brother across from her, beside her sister, a dog at their feet. Mom and Dad at each end. Judy held out her plate which her father took, and Judy nodded, she likewise eager, as Matt and Sally, or Mr. Barkis in Pennsylvania, but Judy was back home, and she said,

"Dad! I'm starving!"

"You don't get *this* up there, do you?"

While he piled her plate full of stuffing and turkey, she frowned, and bit her lip.

"No," she said, in thought, "I get something else, which I

sure as hell didn't get here."

"Don't!" snapped Mom—"start that again!"

Dad laughed, "Sorry, sorry."

But in the sound of his apology and laugh, Asa and myself had followed the two wives into the bar, and we stood behind them, watching closely, something clicked, Judy blinked, and in an echo of his apology, looked at her father. His black hair was shaved close along the sides, as well as on top. His face was clean shaven, his clothes—cotton white and denim blue—clean and pressed, yet as she looked at him, his face changed as clearly Audrey grabbed me, and Dottie Blaze, screaming— LUCKY! YOU ARE *DRUNK*—AGAIN! SMASHED OUT OF YOUR MIND AND MARIO AND HELEN AT HOME WAITING FOR SUPPER!

AND *YOU!* GUY *BLAZE!* WITH MAX AND SEYMOUR BACK IN TOWN, BOTH WAITING FOR SUPPER! *BLAZE!* she swung—in disbelief fixedly Judy stared at her father's close-cropped hair turning white as round steel rimmed spectacles appeared before his curved and heavy-lidded eyes, a sparse western-style mustache appeared below his nose, and as she lowered her plate, she was in shock fright face aghast, hands rose to parted lips slowly—Blaze yelled ASA! as I tried to get away from Audrey's punches, I moved toward the scene—two wives pummeling their husbands—but both stopped, and ASA? WHO IS ASA! Blaze had his face in his hands, and Lucky laughed saying you nitwit, aren't things tough enough? As a matter of fact, I said it was enough in itself, but the storyline had gone overboard. Blaze had just taken a right cross on the snoot from Dottie, and Audrey had slammed Lucky over the head with her handbag literally stunned into silence, Judy— terrified by the transformation before her, froze—.

"This," I said, speaking of myself, "is enough," and they began to vanish to the end as contact with space through one touch of energy, the bars, voices, their figures, fictions, and

110

selves, Blaze and Lucky looking at me in grief, with a plea for more, as puppets to their puppetmaster at the final curtain, yet they as well as the storyteller, dissolved, and as a crash of thunder from soft blue skies marks the end of an illusion I heard a sound, as a whimper from a wounded body—Judy's voice—muted, and in suspense, in the silent reverberation following fresh completion my brain jolts to her murmured Daddy *aw* Nathan streaming, real tears, from soft blue eyes. Not so strange.

No.

Printed January 1981 in Santa Barbara & Ann Arbor for the
Black Sparrow Press by Mackintosh and Young & Edwards
Brothers Inc. Design by Barbara Martin. Cover collage by
Fielding Dawson. This edition is published in paper wrappers;
there are 250 hardcover copies numbered & signed by the
author; and 26 lettered copies handbound in boards by Earle
Gray each with an original drawing by Fielding Dawson.

Photo: George F. Butterick

This is the third novel in a series of five. *Four Penny Lane* will follow, and the last will be *Nickel Street*.

The author was born in New York City in 1930, but grew up in Kirkwood, Missouri. He wrote and drew at an early age, and in 1949, after having graduated from high school, went to Black Mountain College to continue his work, which he did until 1953 when he was drafted. He was a cook in the large Army hospital outside Heidelberg, Germany. In 1955 he returned Stateside, got out of the Army, and not quite a year later came to New York, in May, 1956, where he has been ever since, except for a year in Provincetown, a few months in Vancouver, and brief visits both here and abroad on reading/lecture tours. He is a prolific writer, and has published over 300 stories, essays and criticism in over two hundred magazines and newspapers around the world. He is also an exhibiting artist.

How lively and bright I find his books. He gets the numen of things onto a page.

—*Guy Davenport*

He is the master of Metropolitan Conceit.

—*David Southern*